About the Author

I'm a twenty-something English language teacher. My dry sense of humour is a side effect of being born and raised in Cork, Ireland. I spent eight years working as a hairdresser, until the world came to an abrupt halt in 2020. I studied online and got TEFL certified and moved to Italy in August 2021. I currently live in Milan with my deaf cat, Doja. While I really enjoy teaching, writing is my first real love. Although I have been escaping reality by writing all my life, I started and completed my first novel during the pandemic. Writing helps me with my anxiety, which I've suffered from most of my life. I'm very much into music and sing a little (especially after a few glasses of wine). My taste in music ranges from Bob Dylan to K-pop. I'm working on my second book in my free time.

Who Said it Would be Easy?

Emily O'Callaghan

Who Said it Would be Easy?

Vanguard Press

For Bridget Argue

Acknowledgements

Mom and Dad,

Thank you for believing in me always and supporting my ideas, no matter how crazy they were. Thank you for loving me when I couldn't love myself. Thank you for giving us a home that we can always run to when we are lost.

To my sister, thank you for always having my back. You were always the one in my corner, even when I was totally wrong. Daniel, my brother-in-law, thank you for making my sister so happy. Thank you both for giving me my nephew, Caolan.

To my Milanese family, the ones who inspire me every single day. I value you all more than you know. There were days where I couldn't make it without you, and for you I will forever be grateful. Thank you for never judging me and always supporting me. You helped me regain faith in the world. I will always love you.

To my two aunts, Bernadette and Karen, all my cousins, Amy, April, Aidan, Steven, Cliona and Shane, my uncle Timmy and his wonderful wife Nicola. We put down a hard year without our leading lady. I am glad we have each other. Love you always.

To my only remaining grandparent, Timmy Collins. Although you will never read this, thank you for teaching me that self-belief is the most powerful quality. I love you so much.

Thanks to the girls in Biba. What an amazing group of women. I was so lucky to have met you all. Thank you for helping my through some of the hardest times of my life. You helped me grow up.

To Emma. Though we live so far apart now, nothing ever changed. Thank you for always being my friend, even if, I didn't always deserve it. I love you.

Finally, to those who have had to be brave for far too long, thank you for hanging in there.

Chapter 1

The plane landed with a thump and woke me from my Valium-induced sleep. I needed help getting through the last of my two flights home. Well, I didn't know if I should call it home; it was where my parents lived now. I was going to see them for a month, before I began my new venture with my best friends, Molly and Olivia. We'd just spent a year in Japan, teaching English, and now I was reluctantly coming back to see my parents for a month, before the girls and myself headed off to South Korea for the foreseeable future. I hadn't seen any of my family since I'd left last year. They didn't exactly approve of me leaving to have a life of my own. My dad came into a lot of money five years ago and packed up everything in Ireland and moved to France. He invested in a small vineyard business, which ended up becoming one of the most popular wines, thanks to a certain rapper who was seen holding a bottle on a yacht in Saint Tropez a few summers ago.

I have a tendency to ramble, so bear with me, please.

Anyway, back to my story. I was a little groggy from the flight (Valium and champagne didn't help) and ended up missing the last two steps of the stairs off the plane, so when I say I arrived in France with a bang, I mean the noise my knees made when they hit the tarmac. I was *mortified*. I really wanted the ground to swallow me up. I managed to gather myself and sheepishly headed towards passport control. I avoided making eye-contact with anyone for fear they would ask if I was okay, and I would sooner die than that happen.

Queuing in the thirty-two-degree heat should be considered illegal. If my face got any redder, they wouldn't let me past customs. Fortunately the air con hit me in the nick of time before the makeup started dripping off my face. I'm painting such a cool picture of myself, right?

My sister, her husband, my niece, Alison, and my nephew, Ben, met me at the airport. I could hear Ben screaming before I could see him. I adored them with all my heart. Being away from them was probably the hardest part of the last year. They were eight-year-old twins. My sister and I weren't very close until they were born. I felt like my heart could burst, seeing them again. They both ran to me and almost knocked me over. Why was I so nervous about coming home? It felt amazing receiving those precious cuddles.

I walked hand in hand with my little buddies till we got to the car. My sister always liked the finer things in life, so it was no surprise that her jeep was almost bigger than our childhood home. There was plenty of room for us and all my luggage.

We loaded in the car and began the journey. The drive seemed longer than usual from the airport. The scenery was even more beautiful than in my memories. My parents' house was five kilometres outside of the city of Nice. I loved it there. I think I might have missed it if I allowed myself to.

I was so nervous about seeing my parents again. I wasn't the same person I was when I left. I am not referring to the forty kilograms of weight I'd lost, because that wasn't what was weighing me down, so to speak. I had lost the feeling of expectations that my parents burdened me with, along with the pressure of always being there for them to lean on. There were times when I felt that that pressure was so suffocating that I didn't know if I would ever feel normal again. So naturally I wanted to get as far from that feeling as possible.

We pulled up to the house, and waiting at the door, was my mom, dad and our three dogs. My mom was the most beautiful person I'd ever seen. She had the most amazing silky, straight, black hair, green eyes and sallow skin. Living in France suited her. My dad had black, wavy hair that was sprinkled with a few grey hairs, and sallow, freckled skin. You would wonder where I came from, having such pale skin that I was almost see-through, and golden-blonde hair. I definitely got my eyes from my dad, though: the blue-grey colour was undeniably like his.

My parents glowed in the summer sunshine. They looked healthy and relaxed. It was nice to see after all the years of hardship.

My father was a property developer up until the recession hit, and we literally lost our family home and everything we had. I was seventeen at the time the bad luck arrived, and we put down a hard number of years as a family, until things finally turned around. My mom was diagnosed with rheumatoid arthritis when she was twenty-eight and had to have both knees replaced eventually. The recovery from that was hard, but she was truly soaring now and has never looked back. I struggled a lot with anxiety and depression while all this was going on, and the added dependency of my family on me didn't help matters. I ate badly and often overindulged. When I drank alcohol, I would mostly overdo it. I surrounded myself with toxic people who drained the soul out of me, and every boyfriend I'd had shattered my heart.

I decided, a year ago, to quit the family business and head off to teach English. I could finally put my English degree to good use. It was the best decision I'd ever made. Japan was the most incredible place to reinvent myself, so I came home a completely different girl. At least, that is what I kept telling myself.

While I was away, I met my best friends, Molly Parker and Olivia Lee, and we'd been inseparable ever since. This would be the longest we'd been apart since we'd met, but they would join me in ten days and spend the rest of the time with me in Nice, before we headed to South Korea a few weeks later. Having friends that comforted you on your worst days and celebrated with you on your best, made life worth living.

I met Molly on our first day of orientation, when I walked in on her flirting with the director of the school. (She was adamant that this was why we ended up getting the nicest apartment and why we all got to live together. Olivia reckoned it was because of 'sheer good luck'.) She turned out to be staying in the hotel room next door to me, with a girl she described as a 'wet mop'. She had bright-red hair that matched her fiery personality. She was always quick to call me out on my bullshit. I loved that about her. She was from New York, full of confidence and hated being vulnerable. She was the friend that would always hype you up on your bad days and always said it like it was. Most people didn't quite know what to make of her brash, straightforward and outspoken opinions, but deep down she was soft and the most loyal person I knew. I was immediately drawn to her 'no fucks given' attitude, from the moment we met.

Olivia and I met when we were assigned as roommates for orientation. I introduced her to Molly, and we all sat together from the first lecture onwards. She didn't really get on with Molly at first. She thought she was rude and obnoxious. It wasn't until our second week of training, that Olivia changed her opinion. We went out together and drank too much sake. Olivia vomited on a Japanese businessman's Armani suit, and Molly somehow flirted her way out of us having to pay for it.

She was from New Zealand. The middle of three sisters. The mediator. She was laidback, kind and understanding. Her dark hair and dark-brown eyes complemented her olive skin. She was calm and always looked at everyone's side of view before coming to her own conclusion. She was wise and preferred to 'sleep on it' before coming to a decision. I admired her so much. She calmed me down when I was being irrational, by just looking at me. She was really into nature and 'being at one' with her surroundings. I loved who I was around them both. They kept me grounded and balanced me out.

I sent a text to the group chat once I'd landed.

'Hey my lovelies! I just arrived in France. About to take the shuttle bus straight to hell. Hope you both had safe flights. I wish you were here with me now. I'll be able to survive the next ten days without you guys, right? Love you both. Text me when you make it home. xx'

Olivia immediately replied:

'Hey beautiful. I got home about an hour ago. All is well here. Miss you. You will be fine. Enjoy time with your family. It won't be long till we get there. Love you lots. xxx'

Molly followed suit not long after:

'Hey Bitches. I'm just in JFK waiting for my fucking family to come get me. The flight was a joke. There was a hottie sitting beside me. I spent four hours having drinks and flirting with him before he showed me a picture of his wife and kids. Why is everyone fucking married? I'm now hungover, eating a cheeseburger in arrivals. I don't know what time of the day it is. FML. If I got through that flight, babes, you'll get through the next ten days. If you really need me, I'll gladly get on the first flight out. Love ya ladies. Stay strong, and avoid married men. x'

Reading their texts made me laugh. At least I knew I had the support of the two most important people in my life. It was just my family. Nothing bad could happen. Right? I took two deep breaths and walked up to greet my parents for the first time in a long time.

Chapter 2

The smell of freshly baked bread hit me as I walked into the hallway of the house. I realised just how hungry I was. At least I was at the stage now where my parents couldn't comment on my weight, because I was healthier than ever. So I was definitely going to enjoy the food. More so the wine. I'd been craving a nice, big glass of French wine. I wasn't entirely sure if it was advisable to drink again, with Valium in my system, but I was still alive to tell the tale. Besides, I needed it to get through the awkwardness of being at 'home' again.

It took everything in my power to not be sour about them not once coming to visit me. I kept my head up and my lips sealed. I figured if I ignored my feelings long enough, everyone would be safe.

Everyone seemed happy to see me. I immediately walked through the house and out to the stables to see the horses. That was definitely one thing I missed while away — just the smell of a horse. I know that may sound weird to some people, but I had been horse riding since I was a toddler, and being around them always made me feel safe. They obviously had horses in Japan too, but I was trying to do other things. Avail all opportunities.

The horses were happy inside, away from the heat, in their mildly air-conditioned stable building. Every time I experienced the blast of cool air, it made me laugh at how different life was. Before, there were times we could barely afford feed for the horses, and the bad winters in Ireland took its toll on them. Now they were living in luxury. We all were. Anything we wanted, we got. Which was another reason I wanted to pave my own way in the world. I think struggles were what made you human. Life shouldn't be always good or always bad. There should be balance.

After my catchup I went back inside. The food had to be ready. I was *starving*, and the smells coming from the kitchen were enough to drive me crazy.

We all sat at the long, marble table in the dining room, Ben and Ali on either side of me. I might have mentioned this before, but I adored them. It surprised me how easy this was. All of us together again. Seemingly, all my bad feelings were leaving me. It was nice to catch up with everyone. Listen to what I had missed out on. Although neither of my parents asked me anything about my experience in Japan, and every time I brought something up, they would promptly change the subject. It was weird. To make matters weirder, they offered me the apartment in the city to stay in while I was home. Mom had just had it redecorated. Epic! The girls would love it when they got here. It overlooked the port, and it was a short walk to the restaurant and whiskey bar we owned. I felt silly being so negative about my parents, because they would give me anything material, but what I want from them couldn't be bought.

Dad said he had a car there for me and had to transfer me onto the insurance first thing the next morning. I didn't know what I was so worried about — the next few weeks were going to be epic. Especially with the girls arriving in the next few weeks.

We said our goodbyes, and my sister dropped me at the apartment. I would see them for brunch in Nice tomorrow, so don't feel too bad for them. I was jet-lagged and slightly hungover once my wine buzz wore off, so I said we'd better call it a day. Truth be told, I wanted to get to the apartment, unpack, shower and get into bed. It had been a long forty-eight hours, and I was super excited to see the sun setting over the port. I missed the ocean terribly.

I spent the car journey there telling my sister, Andrea, all that I was planning on doing the next day. Get up early, go for a run, then head straight to the beach for a swim. We were scheduled to meet for brunch at twelve thirty, so that gave me plenty of time for myself first.

"I really want us to go shopping after we eat tomorrow," Andrea said. "I need a whole new wardrobe; I hate everything I own. Everything makes me look like a mother of two."

"Well, you kinda are a mother of two," I said, smirking at her.

"Yeah, well, I had twins, so technically I was only pregnant once," she snapped back at me. "I'm only thirty-one, for Christ's sake; I shouldn't feel middle-aged, but I do," she pouted at me.

"Fine, but you're buying me dinner afterwards. Shopping with you is so stressful, it makes me break out in hives." I smiled sweetly at her.

"Deal. I'll get a babysitter, and we can have a few drinks together afterwards."

The thought of spending alone time with my sister was exciting. We hadn't done anything like that in years. She was definitely getting her groove back.

We arrived outside the apartment. I couldn't help but squeal with delight when we pulled up outside.

Taking my four suitcases out of her car was like a workout in itself. "Fucking hell! Thank god there's an elevator," I sighed, dragging the last one out onto the ground.

A little disclosure: I swear a lot, so if you're easily offended by that kind of thing, it's best you leave now. (It will get much worse as the story continues.)

It still amazed me how I managed to fit my life into four suitcases. Oh, and my carry-on case as well.

"Right! Let's get these bad boys upstairs, shall we?"

The apartment was on the second last floor of the building. It had access to the rooftop also, but we never went up there, as the surrounding balcony was enough if you wanted to sit outside.

My sister went ahead of me, as I was taking in the scenes of the port from the ground floor.

"Come on, for fuck's sake, I want to get home to my babies," she teased.

She made me uncomfortable at how much she was watching me and smirking the whole way up in the elevator. "What's with you?" I asked.

She just giggled and shook her head. The elevator doors finally opened, and we walked in silence to the door of the apartment. "No key is needed now, Dolly. It's an electronic lock. The code is your birthday. I thought that best, in case you were hammered some night and lost your keys," she said, with delight in her eyes.

My family called me Dolly or Ami. I had no idea why. I think it was a joke that only my dad got, but now everyone used it. Unless I was in trouble. Then I was Amelia.

"Oh yeah! Thanks a mill!" I laughed.

We went inside, my life in all four cases, and my hand luggage, behind us.

Chapter 3

The apartment was so modern — way different than I remembered — thanks to Mom's hard work. Not at all her style. She was usually more French country, and she was quite classic. This apartment was way more aesthetic. Very clean and open, and no clutter. Very light. The kitchen was a beautiful, grey colour; very light, with pops of green here and there along the marble countertops. I couldn't wait to cook there. I just wanted to be left alone so I could pass out on the nearest bed, but my sister lingered around like a bad fart.

"Well?" she kept saying. "What do you think of it?" she finally burst.

"It's honestly so beautiful. I love it . It's not Mom's taste at all, which has surprised me. But it's really, really nice."

"Come on, let's go see the rooms," and she dragged me up the stairs. "The first bedroom — the master one — is yours. It has mostly glass for that beautiful view but also loads of light. There's an en suite, walk-in wardrobe/ dressing room down at the end of the room. Go right for the bathroom and left for the wardrobe. I made up little welcome home hampers for you and your friends. They are on the end of each of your beds. There's some pyjamas, slippers, skincare products, night and day creams, sunscreen, makeup removing cleansers, cotton pads, tampons, some candles, shampoo, conditioner, styling products, boob tapes and gel pads for heels. All the essentials," Andrea said, without taking a breath.

"Awh, that's so sweet of you. Your maternal side is really showing," I laughed.

Without a second thought, she grabbed me by the hand and showed me the next four bedrooms, and the living room with a fully stocked bar. There was a built-in wine fridge, a state-of-the-art speaker system and a little piano in the corner. My eyes widened out of pure confusion.

"Perfect for entertaining, right? It's definitely a place for an epic afterparty. Which I will take major offence to if I'm not always invited," she warned me.

She showed me the utility room with all the appliances. The house was prepared with everything I needed. The fridge was stocked with everything I liked. It was so weird and off-putting. I was really appreciative and happy, but there was no need.

Finally we got to see the last room. Apparently I'd never seen this place before, so she insisted on blindfolding me first.

"Come on, Mrs. Grey, let's get this over with! I'm fucking wrecked," I pleaded.

Now that I think of it, who carries a blindfold in their handbag?

"OK, OK, OK. We are ready. Don't let go of my hand, and follow me. In a minute, you're going to have to climb a few steps," Andrea said, as she led me blindfolded around the apartment. "Right now. Here's the steps: one, two, three, four!"

"Yeah, I can actually count. Thanks for the lesson," I said sarcastically.

"Ha, ha! Just shut up, and keep coming. OK, we are here. Ahhhh! Could you take the bloody thing off any fucking slower?" Andrea snapped. "You need to see this."

I uncovered my eyes and tried to make sense of where I was. The rooftop. Dad had a pool put on it. As in, like a swimming pool and a hot tub. What the actual fuck. It was designed so beautifully. There was a little herb garden and fresh tomato plants. A lemon tree. Great! I'd have to remember to water them. A huge built-in barbeque area, and a long table with benches either side of it. I was in shock. Why would they go to such bother when I was only home for the bones of a month?

I slumped down on one side of the benches to try and process this.

"What the fuck is wrong with you?" my sister asked.

"Honestly, I'm just overwhelmed. Our parents hardly spoke to me while I was away, and then I come back to this. Everything I was saying I wanted to have in my dream house, is here. It's all a bit weird," I explained.

"Well, Ami, for someone so smart, you can be a little stupid sometimes. They obviously want you to stay," Andrea said. "Here, let me get you a drink. You look like you could use one." She returned from the kitchen with a glass of wine. After handing it to me, she placed her hands on both my shoulders and looked me dead in the eye. "Please blink, so I know you're still in there," she said. "You have barely reacted at all, and you're the dramatic one!"

"Ha, ha, fuck off! Right, let's try this again," I muttered, after practically inhaling my wine. I pretended to whip off the blindfold

"*Ohhh myyy goddd*! What happened to the rooftop? It's *amazing*. Did Mom and Dad do all of this?" I squealed.

"Yeah, they started two months ago so it would be ready for you to come home and live in."

"*Ehhhh*! What do you mean, to live in?" I asked.

"As in, live in for the foreseeable future. Dad's opened up a new position for you in the vineyard. Since you're multilingual and all, you're going to be a huge help with our overseas buyers."

"Andrea , I'm leaving again in a month, for Korea, to continue teaching. That's my dream," I replied, as politely as possible, while taking her hands in mine.

"Well, I don't know," she said, pulling away. "It's nothing to do with me, anyway. You don't have to make any decisions yet. You're too emotional now. Think about it. Enjoy all the perks while you're here. It will remind you of the good times. I'm going home now. Have a nice bath, climb into bed early, and I'll see you tomorrow."

I slowly followed on behind her, carrying my then empty wine glass.

"I love you. Goodnight!" she shouted from the front door.

I closed the door behind her and slid down onto the floor. *Are they for real? Setting me up in the most amazing way, organising a car for me, doing up the rooftop. Not just that, but also putting in a pool on the roof. All with the intent of bribing me to stay home.* My grip tightened on the glass in my hands. *Fuck this, I need a strong drink!*

I went to the living room bar and poured myself a Jameson and ginger ale with ice and fresh lime: my signature drink. I walked into the bathroom, slumped myself on the edge of the bath and proceeded with my thoughts while the bath filled. *Why on earth are they going to such trouble? I need to experience life on my own and be my own person. I want to see the world. What if they refuse to let me come home ever again, if I say no? What if they actually disowned me or something? And I never get to see the twins!*

My heart started racing, and my cheeks started to get red-hot. I needed to remember my breathing techniques. *Deep breath, in and out. In and out.*

Once the bubbles were almost at the top, I whipped off my clothes, sat in the bath and turned on the TV. With the cocktail in one hand and the remote in the other, I washed my worries off of myself. I thought of my negative thoughts as being printed on my skin, like someone stamped them on there. All I needed was a wash, and they were gone again for another day. That is what I needed.

I popped on a sheet mask and lay in the bath until my fingers resembled a prune. "It's best I get out now," I said out loud, and then I burst out laughing at the fact I was alone.

It was one thing to talk to yourself in your mind, but out loud was another story. I got out, dried off, brushed my teeth and proceeded with my night time skincare routine. A six-step skin ritual may seem like a lot to other people, but I wanted to remain wrinkle-free for as long as humanly possible.

I cleaned up the bathroom, put on my pyjamas and went to put both glasses in the dishwasher. I wandered aimlessly around, looking at the place properly, noticing all the little details. Mom had put so much work into this place. All the homely touches. I came to an abrupt halt when I noticed the pictures on the piano. All were pictures of my family, except one. The last photo at the back was a picture of my ex-boyfriend and I.

What the fuck is wrong with my family! Who's idea was this! Why the fuck would you knowingly put that picture in a frame! Why would this be OK! I screamed to myself hysterically. *OK, I am dramatic. Calm down. It's probably not what I think. Maybe she just forgot we broke up before I left. Maybe she thinks if I see him enough, I'll want to get back together? No. Maybe she thought that because it was taken on such a fun family day out, that I would just want it as a memory? Or maybe it was accidentally in the pile of pictures. Oh, I don't know.*

I was over-exhausted and over-emotional, so it was best I went to bed. My head couldn't take any more surprises. I climbed into bed and smothered myself with the duvet. Before I knew it, I was in a deep, deep sleep.

Chapter 4

I woke up at seven a.m. to my alarm clock screaming at me. I slept like a log. I woke up feeling positive. Nothing or no one could bring me down today. It's the day I was going to get shit done!

First things first. I was going to go for a run on the promenade, and go for a swim after. I got up, got the music pumping in the kitchen and proceeded to get dressed for a run. It was going to be hot today. Once I started rummaging through my suitcases, I knew I should quickly unpack. My room would be a mess otherwise. My dressing room/wardrobe was so perfectly set up, it would be a shame to not use it.

It took me only thirty minutes to unpack everything. I had so much storage, it was crazy. I picked out an off-the-shoulder, black playsuit for brunch later. I paired it with my platform, rose-gold sandals that wrapped up around to the mid-calf, and my rose-gold hoops. I put on rose-gold aviators and my small, Prada backpack. All sorted for later on. Once that was done, I filled my water container, organised a towel for myself and laced up my running shoes. I picked the perfect running playlist while going down in the elevator.

The heat hit me the minute I stepped outside. I threw my beach bag into the car outside so I wouldn't have to go all the way back up, and I could go straight for a swim to cool down.

As I walked onto the promenade, I heard two guys shouting at one another playfully. They were trying to fish off the nearby dock, it seemed. As I continued towards them, I noticed just how handsome they both were. One was really tall — about six foot, I would say — with flawless, honey-toned skin and brown eyes. His hair was light brown (it looked lighter than what it should be naturally) but it was hard to tell under his "I heart Nice" baseball hat.

The other boy, who had skin almost as light as mine, was dressed in all-black, oversized clothes, with a black mask hanging under his chin. His dark eyes peaked out through his messy, black hair that was under a black bucket hat. I couldn't make out what they were saying to each other, because it was in a different language, but they seemed to be teasing one another.

I turned on my heels and began a few quick stretches before popping in my air buds and heading off for my run. I was only planning on doing about two kilometres today. I was on vacation, after all. The scenery was just breathtaking, and the time went by almost too fast.

Before I knew it I was back at the pier, heading towards the car. I looked to see if the boys were there and ended up making eye contact with one of them.

"Excuse me, miss," he said, running up to me.

I got completely flustered. I was red-faced and sweaty from my run. He was so handsome and perfect. *Oh, someone save me.* "Umm, ya! Uh! Yes?" I answered meekly.

"Do you happen to know where we could get iced coffees nearby? And maybe some breakfast? We have been fishing since seven, and we are very, very hungry. We are on vacation." He spoke very confidently.

Avoiding eye contact, I recommended the cafe around the corner. "Are you staying nearby?" I asked.

"Yes. We are staying in that building behind you." He pointed to the same building as the one I was in.

"Oh, cool. I'm staying in the penthouse of the same building," I spat out.

"Good for you," he said, in a way that made me cringe. God, it must have seemed like I was bragging!

He watched me as if he was trying to read my thoughts, and before I could respond, he said, "There are five of us here together on vacation. We are here for a month. We have been travelling around for work for the last year, so we needed the downtime before we return home," he explained.

"Oh, really? That's cool. Where are you guys from?" I asked.

"You really don't know who we are?" He seemed surprised.

Confident just went to arrogant, and now I was pissed off. I finally brought my eyes up to meet his. "Ah, no, should I?"

"Well, we're really famous. You must be the only person who doesn't recognise us," he laughed.

That pissed me off even more. "OK, I'm going to stop you there. The cafe I was telling you about is just around the corner, and as I said before, you can't miss it. I hope you and your 'very famous' friends enjoy your holiday, and if you need any more recommendations, feel free to ask literally anyone other than me. See ya around." I spun so fast, I almost did a one-eighty.

"Goodbye, miss. Thank you for your recommendation. Sorry if I offended you," he said, as I walked away.

I walked back to my car, got my stuff and headed for the beach. As soon as my feet touched the sand, the annoyance left my body. Why were people so obnoxious? It wasn't attractive. I whipped off my shorts and top, revealing my swimsuit underneath. I walked into the water as far as I could and dunked myself under. "*Holy shit!* It's fucking freezing!" I screamed.

Everyone was staring at me. Horrified parents pulled their kids away from me in the water. No matter where you are, screaming 'fuck' at a child is not acceptable. I couldn't help but laugh. "*Je suis désolé,*" I kept repeating, in between bursts of laughter.

The water was beautiful once you were in it. Just the initial shock, when you first got under it, could be a bit much. I swam for a while and then realised how hungry I was. Time for a light breakfast. I gathered my stuff, gave myself a light dry-off and threw on an oversized Tupac T-shirt, which was like a dress on me, and my Givenchy sliders. I headed towards the apartment. I thought, *Why make breakfast when I can buy it?*

I was craving an iced vanilla latte. I wandered over to the cafe I had told that boy about earlier. I went in and got my coffee and a small pastry. I got them to go, as I didn't want to run into them inside.

I was walking aimlessly back to my apartment, when my phone rang and jolted me from my thoughts. It was my sister.

"Hey, girl, I hope you're up. I forgot to tell you yesterday. I booked us in for blow-drys and to have our nails done at ten. Will you be ready? I can meet you at the salon," Andrea said.

"Oh, unreal. That would be fantastic. Thanks so much."

"Perfect. Come dressed for brunch, and we can head there afterwards. I'm bringing Ali with me. She's dying to see you. Ben is with David, having a boys morning. I have to go now, there's another call coming through. Bye, Ami. Love you."

"Bye, bye-bye, bye, bye, bye." That's how Irish people ended phone calls.

I was beaming. What a nice treat to start my day off right. I didn't even have to dry my hair. Whooooooo.

My smile quickly left my face when the elevator doors opened, and I saw the two boys from earlier, in the hallway near my door. Just sitting on a couch chilling, cool as a breeze. *What now!*

"Oh, hi, you're home, finally. We were waiting for you. I think we started off on the wrong foot earlier. I'm Junseo, and this is my friend and colleague, Yungrae." They both put their hands out to shake mine.

"I'm Amelia, but everyone calls me Ami." I shook Junseo's hand first.

"Everyone calls me Jay," he smiled.

I then shook Yungrae's hand. The touch of his pale skin was so soft. His hands felt like they were hard-working hands. The veins were slightly raised.

"I'm Yungrae. Nice to meet you. Sorry about my friend. He is... hmmm... how do you say... working on himself." He laughed.

My eyes immediately met his, and we held our gaze for what seemed like an eternity. Something ran up my spine, hitting like little, tiny jolts of electricity. His dark eyes drew me in. I glanced at his mouth as he licked his perfect lips. I couldn't take me eyes off them. I pulled my hand out of his and gathered myself. He smirked at me. He must have known exactly how he made me feel.

"Your recommendation proved excellent this morning, so we were wondering if you could help us with more things to do. Also, you're the only local we've met who speaks English willingly to us. We haven't met any Korean people yet, so we have to try and use English," Jay said, as I shot him a look of confusion.

"You're from Korea? Ha, ha! How random! I'm moving to Seoul in a few weeks' time. How random is that!" *Shit, I said random twice!*

"Ha, ha, ha. You better start reading up on Korean culture," Junseo said jokingly.

I thought about it some more before blurting out, "So, you're telling me there's five Korean boys staying in the apartment underneath me? Shortly before I move to Korea? Well, if that isn't a sign, I don't know what is." *Wait, there's five of them. Oh, my god.* It finally clicked. I knew exactly who they were. They are in the Korean group that Molly was obsessed with. I knew they looked familiar. And they were staying right below us. This was going to be either epic or a complete disaster.

"Um, yeah, five of us, but we promise not to be too loud or anything. Is that going to be a problem for you, Amelia?" Junseo asked, which brought me back from my thoughts.

"What? Of course not. That's no problem at all. I'd be happy to help in any way that I can." My eyes met Yungrae's again. "I think you boys are going to have a lot of fun here," I said, sounding a little too eager.

He smiled a crooked smile down at me. He was so tall and mysterious. Perfect almost — not real. I was standing there, with my hair dripping wet, no makeup on and the biggest T-shirt mankind makes. But I still didn't want the moment to end.

"How do we reach you when we need you, Amelia?" Yungrae asked.

"Oh right… yeah. Do you guys have WhatsApp or something? I don't have Kakao downloaded yet. I guess you use things like that, right?" I mumbled, staring down at my feet.

"No, that's fine. Give me your phone."

My head shot up so fast I almost gave myself whiplash. He took it from my hand after I unlocked it, Softly lingering his touch on my skin for a second longer than he should have.

I blushed and looked back down at the floor, until he said, "I've created a group chat for you, Junseo and myself. Is it OK for us to text you?" he asked.

I was slightly disappointed that it was like a three-way thing. That confirmed that they only wanted my help as a friend and nothing more. Bit of a blow to my confidence, but whatever. I remembered what I looked like.

"When you meet the others, we can add them in after. Sound good?"

I nodded in response.

"And obviously we will tell you everything you need to know about Korea and teach you a few words in return," Junseo said.

"We also live in Seoul, so you've officially made friends before you've even arrived there," Yungrae said with a smile.

Junseo nodded in agreement and said, "Well, Miss Amelia, we have taken up enough of your morning. We will leave you to the rest of your day. Thanks for your help. We will be in contact soon." They both shook my hand again and left.

Why do they speak so formally at times? They make me feel like I'm an elderly woman. I walked into my apartment and tried to rescue myself from my thoughts. There was definitely something between me and that Yungrae boy, right? He looked at me for a long time and held on to me for a long time. And then friend-zoned me. *Ahhhh! Boys are so confusing!* I looked at my watch. It was nine fifteen. *Fffffuuuucccckkkk!* I had to get in the shower and wash the beach off me, and my hair needed to be clean going to the salon. *Oh, god, and I have to do my makeup. Christ's sake!!*

I pulled myself together and got ready in thirty minutes. I'd have to top up my makeup after my blow-dry, anyway.

I gathered my things and made my way to the salon. My sister met me at the door, with a coffee and a pastry. How did she know I didn't even get a chance to have mine? She was too good to me.

Getting my hair and nails done was such heaven. The girl who looked after me was a friend of mine, Madelyn. So I was at ease with her, anyway. It was so nice catching up with her. I found out that, while I was away, her boyfriend of five years had cheated on her. He is also one of my ex boyfriend's best friends, so, honestly, I'm not surprised. Not one guy in that friend group was decent. I had actually met him through Madelyn.

I convinced her to meet me and my sister for a drink after work, so she could give me all the gory details. After my hair was done, I went and had my nails done upstairs in the beauty section, with my niece/sidekick, Ali. She had to have hers done, too. She was too cute for words. I hope she picked up this habit from me. I would always have my nails done, no matter what. I didn't care if my arm was being amputated, my nails would be pristine.

I went with a classic, bright red, almond shape this time. I think red was definitely a power colour. It gave me confidence, and pairing it with Mac Red lipstick, I felt ready to take on the world.

We met my sister at reception, to show off our fresh talons. "Ali wanted a red like mine, so we could be like twins, too," I explained.

Ali held up her hands and giggled.

"Your hair is beautiful, Andrea. Did you change the colour? The shine off of it is amazing," I said.

She smiled at me and then put on her sunglasses. "I don't even colour my hair, for a start. They simply just washed and blow-dried it straight. This is all natural," she said sarcastically, with a smirk.

My sister had the most beautiful, dark, wavy hair, and all she ever did was straighten it. I'd never understand her.

"Yeah, yeah! Come on! We'll be late, and you know how much our parents love tardiness," I joked.

On the contrary, our parents had been late for everything. You had to tell them to be there a half hour earlier than everyone else. That way, they would arrive on time. We were supposed to meet at twelve thirty p.m., but we knew we wouldn't see them before one p.m.

We headed to the restaurant, hand in hand, with Ali in the middle. We met Ben and my brother-in-law, David, on the way there. It was the cutest thing seeing the twins reunited after time apart. They got so excited to see one another. It was honestly adorable; I hoped they never lost that bond.

All six of us arrived and were taken to our table on the second floor. Shortly after one p.m. my parents arrived, and we all began chatting amongst ourselves.

"Mom, the apartment is amazing! How did you do all that on your own? That must have taken ages."

"Ah, well, I had plenty of help. Your father took care of the rooftop. That was his special project. He sketched the whole thing one night and gave it to the builder and landscaper the next morning. Insisted they have it done for your return," she said proudly.

Dad joined in. "Ah, it was nothing, really. I just explained how important it was, and they happily obliged."

"Well, you both did an exceptional job. Well done, and thanks for allowing me to stay there. The girls are going to lose their shit when they arrive," I said.

"What were you most surprised by?" my mom asked.

"Oh, the pictures on the piano nearly sent me into cardiac arrest," I admitted by accident.

"Oh, yes, I thought it was important that all of us were represented there."

"Yeah, I loved all of them, except the one of me and Rick. That absolutely has to go," I laughed.

Mom's face dropped. "Well, he isn't the worst guy. Yes, he did some questionable things, but it doesn't mean he's a bad guy. He has a good heart. I think he's worth taking another look at. Besides, your father and him still play squash together every week," she announced, just as I was after taking a gulp of water.

I spat it out immediately. *What the actual fuck!"* Ummmm, whaaaaattt? You still in contact with him? I turned to my sister. "And you failed to mention this, why?"

'I'm so sorry,' she mouthed over at me.

"Well, fuck me." I slammed the glass down on the table. "I've heard it all now. What kind of people stay in touch with their daughter's ex who cheated on her multiple times?" I barked. "Not a bad guy! *Ha!* Have you guys not heard of family loyalty, for fuck's sake!" It was hopeless getting too upset over this.

"He didn't do anything to us, Amelia, and he has certainly changed for the better. He's grown into quite a lovely, young man. He's matured a lot since you've been gone," Mom said, almost proudly.

I sat with my mouth wide open, staring at my hands.

"Ahhhh... I hope you're not too upset, Dolly. I tried playing squash with other fellas at the courts, but he's the only one who's good enough to keep up with me," Dad said.

"It's true," David said meekly. "I tried playing against him and threw my back out! He's an intense opponent."

41

Now it started to make sense. All these things were just to soften the blow. My parents philosophy: throw enough money at the problem and hope it will go away.

"You're going to have to face him at some stage, Dolly. The two of you can't move past this if you don't talk things out," my mother said.

"Ah, ya! I wouldn't hold my breath, Mom. That's not what I'm here for. I came to see you guys and relax. I am going to need time to process this. It's beyond weird."

Dad handed me a credit card, with a panicked look on his face. "I don't want you spending your money while you're here. You're to put any and all expenses on this."

I looked over at my sister. She was beaming at me.

"Dad, we're actually going shopping after this. I need to get a few new bits for myself and the kids. They are growing so fast." Andrea nodded towards them.

They were so quiet, colouring at the end of the table. I remembered how many times I'd cursed in front of them today. *I'm such a bad influence!*

"Oh, no problem. Why don't you take the company card and get what you need on that, Andrea."

Andrea looked at me and winked. I could almost hear her thinking: 'If he wants us to spend his money, I suppose we should spend his money.'

Brunch finally ended, and we all said our goodbyes. Dad, Mom and David were taking the kids to the playground for the evening, and David would come to join us for drinks later.

I took my phone out and immediately texted the girls. 'You guys are never going to believe what is going on over here. I can't wait to see you. I am barely surviving without you guys. Can it be next Wednesday already! P.S. there is a major surprise for you here, Mols. Well, technically five surprises… that happen to be staying in my building. Love you both!'

We headed for Avenue Jean Medecin to spend some euros. We hit Zara and H&M first. Then we went to Massimo Dutti, Chanel, Armani, and finally, Loui Vuitton. I bought plenty of bags and shoes. I bought a white Gucci bucket hat and a white beret. All essentials, really. I bought a few different outfits for going out while I was here. For dinner that night, I bought a green skirt and crop top co-ord to wear with the Chanel gold chain belt and gold sandals. I wasn't not so much into labels, normally, but I was pissed off and charging it to my father's account, so I thought, 'what the hell.'

Hours went by like minutes. Shopping was actually fun. My sister wasn't half as annoying as she normally would be.

The rumbling noise coming from my stomach alerted me to check the time. "It's five p.m. already? The day flew!"

Andrea looked surprised. "Wow! I made reservations for us at six thirty in the bar. I've been dreaming about wine all day! We would want to get rocking! Let's head back to your apartment, wash up, change, top up the faces and head over there. I am gasping," she joked.

I tried talking to her all day about what had happened at brunch, but she kept distracting me. I knew once she had a few drinks and relaxed, I could bring it up then.

We got back to the apartment in no time. I spied two more of those Korean boys in the lobby of the building. I smiled politely at them and watched as their eyes widened when they saw how much stuff we had. We somehow managed to fit us and all our shopping into the elevator.

I was praying they couldn't hear my sister as she said in the loudest possible way, "Ami, Who... were... they? So handsome. They look awfully familiar. They must be in that band all the locals are talking about!"

The doors of the elevator closed finally.

"The girl in Chanel told me about all about them. Apparently she's a huge fan — been following them for ages. Anyway, how exciting! Are they staying in your building? Oh, my god. They must be! How random is that? You're moving to Korea. Ha, ha! The world is such a small place! I wonder if they have girl..."

"Andy, *please*," I snapped. "I'm trying to key in the code to open the damn door, and I can't concentrate with you talking like roadrunner."

"All right! Someone is hangry."

We both burst out laughing. While getting ready, I tried to explain what had happened that morning. I told her everything, but I wasn't sure just how much she heard because she had the music cranked up so loud. A few moments passed and not one word from her. I wanted advice. Was I crazy? She got up, disappeared out of the room and returned a while later with two drinks.

She pulled me onto my bed and sat opposite me.

"Right, so," she said, sitting back into the arm chair.

"Right, what?"

"Ami, we need to make a plan of action. I could the excitement in your voice, talking about that boy this morning."

"Two boys. I met two boys."

"Yes, but your voice changed when you mentioned the one in all black; what did you say his name was — Sunray?"

"Yungrae."

"Right, sorry. Yungrae. He made an impression on you. I can tell. Your eyes light up when you say his name. We can't just sit back and do nothing. You need to follow up on that feeling. See if there's more. I personally think the stars are a lining for you. This is too big of an opportunity to pass up on. I remember the darkness that surrounded you when you were with that prick, Richard! He is a major dickhead! I don't care what our parents feel about him. I am sorry I didn't tell you myself, but I didn't realise she was still hell-bent on reuniting you both."

"Andy, I still can't believe our parents are friends with my ex-boyfriend. How fucking weird and dysfunctional is that!"

We both burst into laughter.

"Ahahahahahaha. This is definitely one for the books. Who would believe that shit," Andrea said, tears starting to build in her eyes from laughing.

"If I don't laugh, I'll cry. Andy. It's so weird."

"Anyway... Ugh! I can't stop laughing. Anyway, let's make a plan on what we should do about the guy underneath you."

Our eyes met, and we started giggling again.

"Fuck's sake, we've only had one glass of wine and we're howling. I suppose laugh lines are better than frown lines," I said. "Let's finish getting ready."

Chapter 5

Two glasses of wine and a lot of laughs later, we arrived at the bar my father owned, called 1967. It also did food — mostly tapas and that kind of thing. We were greeted by Hugo, the manager, who brought us to our table on the top floor. The top floor was an open rooftop which was always buzzing with people. I loved it up there. Weeknights in the summer were just as busy as weekends.

David was sitting there waiting for us, looking bored as he finished the end of his second bottle of cider. "Finally, I was getting worried," he sighed. "What are we drinking ladies?" He summoned a member of staff.

"I best stick to the grape; it's too early for the grain," I joked. "Will we get a bottle of prosecco or something?" I asked.

Andrea's eyes lit up. "It's Dom or nothing, little sis."

"Oh, for fuck's sake, when did we get like this? Remember scraping euros together to get shots, when I first started going out," I said.

"Ami. Please. Don't even try to remind me! I still can't drink sambuca! We are just much more fortunate these days. Stop fighting it. It must be exhausting. The past is the past. The present is champagne, and we could be swimming in it," she joked.

"OK, let's just promise to remember where we came from. The higher we climb, the harder the fall."

"All right, Gondi, drink your champagne," David said.

We ordered a table-load of tapas, and we filled in David on everything while we ate. Madelyn joined us somewhere between bottle two and three. My sister and I were in shock hearing all about her breakup with Lucas.

"That's fucking awful. What an absolute dickhead. What is actually wrong with that group of boys!"

"We will never know, Andrea. Maybe it's like a cult thing — a cheaters circle or something," Madelyn joked. "I'm fine now. I promise. It was difficult at first, but I have come to terms with it. Just like Amelia. We will come back stronger."

She squeezed my hand. My phone buzzed. It was Molly: 'Hey girlie! I fucking miss you. My family are driving me nuts. Looking forward to seeing you and finding out about this surprise. Hope things are OK with you. Should we facetime once, before we join you? The time differences are a nightmare. All my love.'

"Right, we promised no phones, Amelia." Andrea snatched mine out of my hand and put it on the far side of the table. "Everyone, pile up your phones here. We can have them back at the end of the night."

"Oh, whatever, I'm going to the bathroom to fix my face."

"Oh, me too, Ami. I haven't touched my makeup since nine a.m. this morning," Madelyn said.

You never knew just how tipsy you felt until you went to the bathroom, on a night out. I was buzzing. We chatted aimlessly about makeup brands while touching up our faces and then finally joined Andrea and David back at our table. Andrea was smiling shamelessly at me, non-stop, for about two minutes, before I asked her if she was having a stroke or something.

"Ha, ha. No. But I did do something while you were away. Your phone buzzed again, and I thought it might be important…"

"Andy, what the fuck did you do now? You're getting as bad as Mom, with the boundaries."

"So, you got a text in the group chat."

"Which one?"

"The one the Korean boy created." Her smile got bigger and bigger.

"Yes, and?" I growled.

"Well, Yungrae wanted to know where would be a nice place for them to get a drink. They want somewhere that they won't be hounded, so I asked Hugo to start moving people downstairs discreetly, and they will be here in ten minutes."

My heart sank in my chest. "Why the fuck did you do that? Fuck, if I thought I would be meeting them, I wouldn't have worn this outfit. Fuck's sake, Andy. I'm never telling you anything again."

"Shut up! You look incredible! I know you. You're secretly delighted. I can see them eyes light up."

I started smiling. "OK. I'm slightly freaking out a little. I need a shot asap."

David immediately got up and jogged towards the bar. He came back with a tray of Patron, salt and lemon slices. "Knock two of these back, and you'll be fine! Come on, we will join you! All together! Everyone!" David urged us.

The alcohol we poured down our throats somehow filled us with a sense of purpose — like we were invincible. Even so, I still felt panicked. I went back and forth over my outfit, my makeup and my hair, in my head. I fussed over what I would have done differently if I knew he was coming. I guess you could say he had had an effect on me, but I tried to publicly deny that. I tried to pretend that I didn't care, but my heart was in my mouth. All I could focus on was the rhythm of my heartbeat in my head. Minutes must have passed and I hardly noticed, anticipating the arrival of the subject of my thoughts. I wondered how he would act around me with more of his friends with him. *Does he even like me? Will he like my outfit? Oh, for Christ's sake, pull yourself together! You don't even know him. He's probably a prick, and he may not even fancy you. Get a grip!* I kept fighting with my thoughts.

Finally Hugo appeared with five extremely handsome boys in tow. My heart raced faster than Michael Schumacher on steroids. *This is it. Breathe. In and out. Be* cool. *Be calm. Be collected.* I focused solely on my breath. I felt my chest rise and fall. Over and over. Until, finally, they arrived at our table. Hugo had summoned the other staff, and they joined tables to ours as fast as possible. My eyes were glued to him. I gazed at him like a child in a sweet shop. I scanned him from head to toe. His black, ripped jeans. His shirt was unbuttoned a little, exposing the top of his bare chest. I had to pry my eyes off his exposed collarbone, so I tried focusing his face. He stood as if he was waiting for permission to sit, so naturally my sister signalled for him to take the seat nearest to me. My heart was full-on in my throat. I was unsure if I could speak.

"Nice to see you again. What are you drinking? I'm so thirsty."

My eyes shot up to meet his. "Um. Ah. Well, we started on champagne. But uhh, there was also some tequila involved," I stammered.

"Ha, ha, ha. Is it starting to kick in, or do I make you that nervous?"

"Probably both," I admitted.

"Good, I was worried that I didn't make enough of an impression on you."

I blushed hard.

"Well, anyway, I better introduce you to the rest of the boys. Everyone, this is Amelia."

They started to introduce themselves, one by one.

"Hello, everyone, I'm Junseo."

"Hey, I'm Yungrae."

"Hi. I'm Jiseok. Nice to meet you."

51

"I'm Taehwan. And this is Daeshim. He's the youngest, so he's a little shy."

They were all so perfect. Each had their own unique style.

"Hey! I'm Amelia. This is my sister, Andrea, her husband, David, and my friend, Madelyn."

"You're much prettier than Yungrae described you. He's been talking about you all day," Taehwan said, with a cheeky smile.

"Ahhhh, OK! That's enough sharing! Thank you so much for that," Yungrae snapped at him. His perfectly pale skin started to flush a little pink. "Let's get some drinks. Please."

My sister immediately said, "Ami, why don't you order this round? I'm sure Yungrae will help you carry them back!" Her face lit up like a child at Christmas.

"Yeah, of course. I'd be happy to. Just point me towards the bar." I rolled my eyes at Andrea as she waved me on from across the table.

"Right! What does everyone want?"

"I'm going to stick to the champagne. You too, Maddie? David, will you have a beer? What about our special guests? What will you all have?" Andy taking control once again.

"We all like champagne!" Daeshim piped in, and gave me two thumbs up.

"Perfect, nice and simple." I turned on my heels and headed towards the bar. Yungrae followed me. I slowed

52

down so we were walking side by side. He was so much taller than me.

"Will we have a few sneaky shots up here? I want to try and catch up with you. It seems like fun," he laughed. "And I know they do table service, but I wanted us to have some alone time, so let's not go back too soon." He smiled down at me.

"OK, but I have to warn you, if you're trying to get me drunk, I'm Irish. I've a good tolerance for alcohol."

"I don't know if you know this, but I'm Korean. We are really good at drinking." He stopped and then said, "Let's place a bet! First one to get drunk enough and stop making sense has to buy the other dinner."

My eyes widened. Anything to spend more time with him, but I was not losing this. "That sounds like a real win-win situation, but yes! Deal. Let's shake on it."

He shook my hand and held it a little longer than he needed to. It was nice. I turned to face Hugo who was waiting patiently for me to order. I didn't even notice he was there until he cleared his throat. "What will it be, my love?"

"Ugh. Ah. Sorry, Hugo. Can we get a pint of Stella, five bottles of Dom Perignon, and some glasses for the table, please. And we need two tequilas for us here."

"No problem, honey. I'm assuming it's Patron again. I need to start doubling my orders when you come home." Hugo winked at me.

"You must come here a lot? To be that comfortable with the bartender, I mean," Yungrae said, looking a little disappointed.

I didn't like his tone. I was taken aback. My insecurities kicked in again. He must think I'm some sort of trashy party girl. "Well, yeah, I've spent a good bit of time here. I worked here for a while when we first opened it. Hugo is like family."

"What do you mean 'we'? You own this place?"

"Well, my family does. My father bought this building a few years ago. It was a dump before. Hugo and my father have turned it into a successful business."

"Yes, I am the flamboyant manager you'll hear lots about," Hugo interrupted. "If you need anything, don't hesitate to ask. Here are your drinks. Enjoy."

Yungrae pulled a black card out of his pocket and insisted on paying.

"No way extremely handsome boys like you should ever pay for anything. Especially when you're making our little Ami here smile brighter than I've seen in a long time. Tonight, everything is on the house," Hugo said and pushed a shot glass in my direction.

"Actually, both of these are for the handsome boy to my left! He's got some catching up to do. I'll have a Jameson and ginger ale, please, Hugo, when you're ready."

"Make that two, that sounds interesting," Yungrae said, while wiping the tequila from his lips. He threw back the second one like it was nothing.

54

Hugo returned with our drinks and promptly left us alone again. I swirled the lime around my glass with the straw, trying to keep my cool. I could feel his eyes on me at all times. "So, you want to tell me more about yourself?"

"Well, I haven't mentioned it before, but I'm Korean. Extremely handsome, apparently. I'm twenty-nine. I have an older brother. I'm big into music. That's how I make a living. My favourite colour has always been black, but recently I'm starting to be really drawn to blue."

"Really? Why blue all of a sudden?" I asked, without hesitation.

He started at me intensely and said, "Well, honestly, I haven't been able to stop thinking about your eyes since I first saw them. Your eyes are blue, right? You're not wearing contacts? I will feel so stupid if you are wearing contacts."

"Ha, ha. No contacts. That's the way they made me." I shyly looked down at my glass again. "You're making me shy, you know," I admitted.

"You have a similar effect on me, you know. I wanted the ground to swallow me up earlier when the boys told you that I was talking about you all day."

"Oh, yeah, I don't know what about the way I looked this morning made that kind of impression on you. Red-faced and wet. Not my finest hour, I have to say."

"You're too hard on yourself. You need to see yourself through my eyes. You are the most beautiful girl I've ever seen. And the Tupac T-shirt was just the icing on the cake. I will want to see that again."

I laughed so hard I almost spilt my drink. He laughed with me.

"Tell me more about yourself, Amelia. I want to know everything. This drink is delicious, by the way. I think it might be my new favourite."

"I'm glad. It's mine, too." I proceeded to tell him about my family and our life in France. I told him about working for the family business after college and all about how my parents were trying to get me to stay here.

He sat and listened. He was so good at listening. We decided to head back to the others. Everyone seemed to be getting on swimmingly.

It wasn't long before Andrea suggested that we play Kings. For those who don't know, this is an epic drinking game that doesn't leave any player sober. Why she had a deck of cards in her bag was beyond me. She darted off to find a glass big enough to be the 'kings cup' and returned with some sort of beer glass that could hold a litre.

"Right, guys, the rules are simple. Each player picks a card, and each of the cards have a different meaning. You don't need to memorise them; we will tell you what means what. Whoever draws a king card has to add some of their drink into the king's cup in the middle. Whoever draws the last king card has to drink the entire contents of the king's cup, and the game is over. Happy drinking, everyone."

Andrea was howling at that point. The game went on for what seemed an eternity, until finally David pulled the last king card. We were all sufficiently hammered at this point and decided to call it a night. We all headed back to the apartments. I suffered a slight wobble when I hit the cobblestone street near our building, but Yungrae grabbed me and held my hand for the rest of our walk. It was nice. All of us were happily nattering to one another. We said goodbye to Maddie as she got a taxi from the front of our building. Poor girl had work in the morning. I didn't know how she was going to manage. Andrea and David were struggling to hold each other up as we keyed in the code to the front door. The elevator wasn't big enough for all of us, so we divided up into groups. Yungrae, Jiseok and Junseo stayed behind with me while the others piled into the elevators and headed upstairs. I sat on one of the couches in reception, and Yungrae plopped down beside me, grabbing my hand from my lap. The way he brushed my skin with his thumb sent tingles all over my body. I was getting addicted to this feeling. I wanted to stay there forever. I lay my head on his shoulder and closed my eyes. I wanted as much physical contact with him as possible.

"Are you OK, Ami?"

I felt his other hand sweep over my cheek and along my jawbone. "Never better."

"Let's get you up to bed." He stood up and offered both his hands to me to pull me up off the couch.

The four of us entered the elevator. The journey up seemed shorter than usual. We were at their floor before I knew it. The other two boys walked out after giving me a hug goodnight. Yungrae stayed with his back pressed to the wall, staring at me, up and down. I must have been blushing so hard; my cheeks felt so hot. The elevator dinged open, and we walked out to my door.

"I had the most fun tonight, Amelia. I'm so glad we met you. I was jealous that I wasn't the first to talk to you, but luckily I am the one showing you to your door now. I hope that's OK. I just wanted to see you got in OK. That's not weird, is it? It's just the way I was raised. I wouldn't sleep well knowing that I didn't see you to your door.". He was rambling.

Oh, god! Was he as nervous as I was? "I think you're going to have to come in for a nightcap. We both seem to be as drunk as the other. We still have a wager. Remember?"

His eyes shot towards mine. "Me, come into your place? Is it a bit soon for you? We only just met?"

"When I say a drink, I mean a drink! OK? I take my bets very seriously!" I crossed my arms and pouted. "I don't want to be one of your groupies, and besides, my sister and her husband are in there!"

He burst out laughing. "Trust me, Amelia, you're anything but a groupie. I don't even think you're a fan. You didn't know us when we first met!"

He continued laughing as I opened the front door and dragged him in behind me. He followed me into the study and sat at the piano. "Wow, I didn't know you played." He started fiddling with the keys.

"Well, Yungrae, we've only just met. There is a lot of things you don't know about me. What do you want to drink?"

"Whatever you're having is fine. I trust you."

"What the fuck is going on in here? A piano recital? I expected you two to be at least making out by now?" Andrea said, bursting into the room, with David giggling behind her. "We will all have one of what you're having, Ami! Thanks for offering."

"Thank you for your outburst, Andy. Make us feel super awkward, why don't you!"

"We are waiting for the pizza guy, bro. We weren't eavesdropping on purpose, or anything" David stammered.

Yungrae laughed. "That's OK, man. I hope you plan on sharing the pizza. I am starving all of a sudden."

"Right, everyone out of here before we break something. Let's go into the living room and look up the boys' music videos."

Yungrae's face dropped. "Oh, no. Really? I'm shy."

I handed him his drink. "Here's some liquid courage. You'll be fine." I smiled up at him.

"Fine. But I get to pick which ones we watch," he said, as I led him into the living room.

Chapter 6

The sound of my phone ringing jolted me awake. What time was it? My mouth felt like I had swallowed a barrel of sand. I felt around the bed till my hands found it.

I cleared my throat. "Ah... ahem... hello."

"Hey, girl, it's Liv. I just thought I'd give you a quick call before bed. It's ten a.m. there, right?"

"Oh, hey. How are you doing? I am hungover. If you didn't call me, I would have slept the whole day, I'd say."

"Awh, shit! I'm so sorry to have woken you! What time did you finish up? What did you even do? I didn't know you were having a wild night out. Isn't it midweek?"

"You're fine. Don't worry; I appreciate you waking me. I would have been so upset with myself if I slept any later. I went to dinner with my sister, her husband and my friend, Madelyn, last night. It unintentionally turned into a major piss-up. There was a king's cup involved. I don't remember going to bed. Ugh. I feel so rough."

"Right, OK. I'm going to let you go. Get yourself some painkillers and lots of water, and I'll call you at the same time tomorrow morning, OK? We can chat then, when you're feeling better. I can't wait to see you. Love you."

"Perfect. We will talk then. Thanks. Love you. Bye."
I threw my phone to the opposite side of the bed. "Water,
I need lots of water." I always keep a bottle beside my bed.

I polished that off and went to have a shower and get
dressed. As the water ran over me, I tried to piece the end
of the night together. I remembered the pizza coming and
all of us dancing and singing in the living room. OK, cool.
I remembered making three more drinks for everyone. OK.
I remembered putting Andy and David to bed. Right. I
remember aggressively asking Yungrae why he still hadn't
kissed me, and then, blank. Nothing after that. Oh, god. I
ran to get my phone and immediately started going through
my calls and messages. Fuck, what did I say or do?

The first message I opened was from Junseo. 'Hey,
Amelia. Is Yungrae still with you? His phone must be off?'

Fuck! What time was that sent at? Nine thirty a.m.
OK, don't panic until you know more! Remain calm. I
sheepishly wandered down the hallway and checked the
other bedrooms. No sign of anyone. All the beds were
made. Fuck. I crept downstairs and went to the living
room. That's the last place I remember being. Nothing.
The place was cleaned up. Surely I was in no state to clean
up after us? I heard laughing coming from the kitchen,
which jolted me out of my thoughts. I slowly peeped
around the door, only to be greeted by the sight of three
other extremely hungover humans.

"Well, good morning. Glad you're alive. You look
fine! Why don't you look as bad as the rest of us?"

"Morning. Ugh, I don't know! I feel horrible, if that helps. I just showered and got dressed. Sorry I overslept."

"What time did you put us to bed? I vaguely remember talking to you in the bedroom we slept in!"

"It was around five a.m. I don't remember much after that, if I'm honest," I said, searching for a reaction from Yungrae. I was trying so hard to figure out if we argued or not, that I just noticed he was cooking breakfast. "You're cooking? Wow. I'm sorry, I just realised. I'm a little slow today. Forgive me."

"It's the least I could do after passing out on your couch." He smiled at me. "This is almost ready. There is fresh orange juice in the fridge."

"Fresh orange juice? Where did that come from?"

"Yungrae made it," Andrea boasted on his behalf.

He blushed and nodded at me. "I hope you don't mind that I rooted around in your kitchen."

"Oh, of course not. Feel free to make breakfast for me anytime." Shit. Why did I just say that?. I slipped onto the chair and placed my head in my hands at the table.

"Food is ready. Great. We will all feel better after this."

I doubt I could feel any worse. I was in the worst fear possible, but at least he was still speaking to me. For those who don't know what 'the fear' is, it's that state of anxiety that one can be in after a night of overdoing it on the booze. The flashbacks make you shudder, and you're afraid to leave the house in case you meet someone who knows what you've said or done the night before. Sometimes 'the fear' can last a few days, and sometimes you can be in 'the super fear', which is much, much worse.

I shamelessly ate every bite that was on my plate. "That was delicious. Thank you so much, Yungrae. Best surprise to wake up to."

He winked at me from across the table. "You're more than welcome. As I said, it was the least I could do."

"Well, guys, this was beautiful, but we better drag our sorry asses home to our children. Thanks for such a fun night. We should do it again before you leave, Ami."

I followed them to the door to say goodbye. "Andrea, what makes you so sure I'm still going to Korea? You seemed convinced I would stay home all along?"

"Baby sis, I saw it in your eyes last night when that beautiful boy walked in. Your heart is already on its way there."

I stood in the hallway, contemplating what she just said. Was she right? No. It just was not possible. We hadn't as much as kissed. *Oh shit! He is still in the kitchen.* I quietly entered the room and began cleaning up.

"Here, let me help you, Amelia."

"Jesus, no way! You cooked, and it was beautiful. Thanks, again. All I have to do is load the dishwasher. No big deal."

"OK. If you insist. I guess we should talk about last night? I had a lot of fun!"

"Um... yeah... I guess we should. The last thing I remember is starting an argument with you. After that, everything is a bit of a blur, I'm afraid."

His face fell. "Oh right... yeah... So you don't remember going to bed, either? OK. Well, we actually didn't argue at all. You scolded me for not kissing you, and then..."

"And then what?"

He looked so disappointed. "And then I kissed you, but nothing else happened. I helped you to bed. It obviously wasn't as memorable for you as it was for me, but at least I won the bet! You owe me two dates."

I slumped down on the chair, speechless. In my mind, I was screaming, 'Are you fucking kidding me?' over and over, but on the outside I just stayed silent, staring at the floor.

"I am so sorry, Amelia. Are you OK? I must have totally misread the situation. Things like holding hands in public obviously mean something different to me. I am so sorry. You must be disgusted."

His response startled me back to reality. "Wait. You think I didn't want to kiss you? It's the one thing I haven't been able to stop thinking about since we met. I am so disappointed that I got too drunk to enjoy it."

His smile widened as he walked over to me and grabbed my face gently in his hands, bringing my gaze to meet him. "How are you feeling now? Better? More importantly, are you sober?"

"Yes, and I would really appreciate it if you kissed me," I admitted.

Before I knew it, his lips were on mine. Gentle but firm. His hands wandered down to my elbows, and he pulled me up until we were both standing upright. His hands then went to my waist, and he pulled me close to him. He continued to kiss me gently. I felt that if he let go of me, I would crumble into pieces. My hands wandered up his strong arms until I reached his hair, which I gently pulled to have him as close to me as possible. Time must have stopped. Kissing him was the only thing I wanted to do from then on.

As things started to heat up between us, he pulled away. "I need to stop before the man in me takes over." He pecked my lips three times before releasing me from his grip.

"Woah," I said, sitting back down, trying my best to come to terms with how much I enjoyed that. I never knew kissing could feel so good. "You're good at that, you know."

He laughed his perfect laugh. "Thanks. I really hope you remember that kiss, because I will never forget it."

I looked at him, baffled. The words were out of my mouth before I could stop myself. "You're this super-famous, incredibly talented musician. You're tall, kind and extremely handsome. You could have anyone in the world. I don't understand how kissing me could be so special." *Oh shit! I sounded so insecure there. He is going to run for the hills.*

He bent down in front of me and put his hands on my knees. "Amelia, I have never met someone that has made such an impression on me like you have. You're so open and friendly. You're so beautiful. You're smart and thoughtful, and you made us all feel so welcome. I could get in a lot of trouble for being so public with you last night, but I really didn't care. I wanted to spend as much time as possible with you. It took everything I had not to grab you and kiss you in the elevator, but I have to be so careful. If you were just a random girl, it probably wouldn't have mattered as much, but I want to protect you. Some of our fan base are really intense. If they found out about you and knew I was here with you, your social media would be open season for them. I need to protect you from that. You wouldn't deserve any of it, and it's so selfish of me, but I can't stay away from you. Saying it out loud, it might seem crazy, but I feel like we were supposed to meet. I feel so at ease with you. It just feels right."

I put my hands on his. "I know exactly what you mean. You have made the same impression on me. Being around you just feels natural. Like I've done it my whole life or something."

"I normally feel emotionally drained after our tours, and I want to rush home and be around my family until I feel better. You know… to ground myself again. It takes a lot out of me. I'm not the most outgoing guy. I sleep as much as I can after a tour, ordinarily. But after the night I've spent with you, I feel recharged, ready to take on anything! And I only got a few hours of sleep."

Hearing his confession made my heart want to burst. "I can't tell you exactly how happy that has made me feel right now. I feel very similar. I think we need to make a pact to just be totally upfront with each other, because we haven't got a lot of time together and we need to make the most of it."

"Amelia? Are you not moving to the city I live in, soon?"

"Yes, but I think logically. We should spend the time that you're here getting to know each other more. It will only get harder for us when we get there. We need to be a hundred percent sure about one another. It's all lovely being in this bubble now, but think of all the hardships down the line."

"That's kinda negative and it's killed my vibe a bit, but yes, you're right. My head is starting to hurt. All those whiskeys are catching up on me."

"Would it be weird if we went for a nap?" I asked.

"Are you kidding me? That would be awesome. Let's go." He kissed me quick and grabbed my wrist, dragging me to my room.

Once we got to where my bed was, he pulled back the covers and ushered me to get in. I lay down, and he tucked the blankets in around me like a child. I giggled so much. I expected him to walk around to the other side, but he surprised me by heading towards the door again.

"Where are you going?" I asked sharply.

"Back to the living room for a nap." He looked at me, confused.

I patted down on the other side of my bed. "Come here. I want to nap with you; that was the whole point. Stop being prince charming and get in beside me, please."

"You sure?"

"Of course, hangover cuddles are the best." I was far too hungover to want anything more than that. If the time came that things went further, I didn't want to feel like death.

He got in beside me, and we talked more about his family and what work was like at that moment. I lay on his chest, listening to him. I could do that forever. I felt so safe at that moment. His breathing started to change and before I knew it, he was fast asleep. I gently kissed his lips and cuddled up beside him before drifting off myself. For the first time in a long time, I was so happy to be home.

Chapter 7

The constant ringing of the doorbell woke us both out of our sleep. I was so confused. I didn't even know there was a doorbell. I reluctantly dragged myself out from under the duvet.

"Don't move," I insisted. "That could be my parents, and I couldn't even begin to explain this."

I hurried to the door and opened it immediately. I was almost smacked by the hand that was banging on the door. I ducked just in time.

"Where the hell is Yungrae? What did you do to him? We haven't heard from him since last night!"

"Ugh, calm down, we were asleep! He's in my bedroom."

Junseo, Daeshim and Taehwan were now standing in my hallway, with shocked expressions. Before I had a chance to answer, Yungrae appeared beside me, pulling his jacket on.

"Where the hell were you? Your phone's been off all morning. We were in such a panic, we almost called our manager." Junseo's face was getting redder and redder with temper.

Yungrae stood smirking at him. "Calm down. I'm fine. We just stayed up late, drinking. No big deal."

"I texted Amelia this morning, and she read it and didn't reply. I thought the worst had happened."

Oh shit. I completely forgot. Everyone was now turned towards me, expecting an explanation. "I'm so sorry. I was so confused when I woke up. I meant to reply once I knew where everyone was. I didn't expect Yungrae to still be here, let alone be in my kitchen, cooking us breakfast."

Yungrae stared at me. "You thought I'd just have left without saying anything?"

"Well, see, I didn't remember going to sleep, so for all I knew, you could have," I said, looking down at my feet.

He laughed, walked over to me and cupped my face in his hands. "That's why you looked so relieved. You're adorable."

He kissed me and pulled me in for a hug. I felt the rattle in his chest as he laughed.

The other three boys stood smiling at us. It was starting to get awkward.

"Anyone want a coffee?"

All four boys immediately answered, and we walked into the kitchen. They chatted away while I made iced coffees.

I handed one to each of them, keeping Junseo's hostage. "Are we good now?"

"Yes. Of course. Just text me back next time, please." He stretched his hands towards me.

I handed him his coffee. "Deal." I smiled sweetly at him and sat down beside Yungrae.

"So, when are you both going to give us all the hot details of last night's escapades?" Taehwan asked excitedly.

"Shut up, Tae," the boys yelled in unison.

"There's nothing to tell. I had too much to drink, tried starting an argument with Yungrae and had to be put to bed."

"Yeah. Yeah. As if I believe you. You both just got out of the same bed, right?"

Fuck. I forgot I had let that one slip. My cheeks started to burn up.

Yungrae put his hand on my knee and squeezed gently. "That's enough interrogating. I need you guys to get along."

Junseo changed the subject and told us how much fun he had last night. His stories seem to go on forever . We finished our coffees, and they got up to leave.

Yungrae stayed back while the boys left. He was gathering up the cups. "I'm sorry about them," he laughed.

"Honestly, it's fine. They are hilarious. I enjoy their banter." I was wiping down the countertops when I felt his breath on my neck. I turned to face him. He was so close to my face, his arms on the counter, caging me in. I couldn't move, even if I wanted to.

"So, there's nothing to tell, eh? Maybe taking things slow isn't a good thing. I want to leave an impression on you," he mumbled, hoovering his lips over my cheek, over my lips and down my neck.

I stood frozen, waiting for him to make contact with me, but he didn't. He began to move away from me, so I grabbed his arms and placed them back at either side of me. I ran my hands up his strong arms and eventually stopped on his face, before pulling him in for a kiss. He moaned against my mouth. His hands ran down my back until he picked me up and placed me on the countertop. I wrapped my legs around his waist. I wanted to feel him against me. The kiss sped up. I could feel his heart beating against my body. I wanted him so badly that I couldn't think straight.

He pulled away from me, and I was just about to try to remove his shirt, when he said, "I think we should stop. I want our first time together to be more special than a quick bang on the kitchen countertop. You said it yourself — we should get to know each other. I don't want sex to cloud your judgement."

"Well, stop teasing me then. I can't help myself. The tension builds and I can't think straight."

"My point exactly."

"Ugh, fine. You are making me out to be some sex-crazed lunatic."

He laughed at me. "I know you're not, but your hormones can get the better of you. I've heard all the stories about foreign girls."

I stared at him, raising my eyebrow, and I pushed him away. "And what about us *'foreign girls'*?"

"Well, some of my friends have been with foreigners. You guys treat relationships differently to us. You get swept up in the fantasy and then bored, or things get rocky, and you dump us out of nowhere."

I didn't like the word 'us'. I didn't like it at all. "Please don't put me in a category like that when you don't even know me. That might have been the case for your friends, but at least know me before you judge me. Not all foreigners are like that. And please don't be like 'them' and 'us'. We are all human. It's very unfair, and frankly, you've pissed me off now. I think you should go."

He looked stunned. "Ami, I'm so sorry. You've picked me up wrong. I didn't mean it like that. Please forgive me." He bowed his head, placing his hands on my thighs.

I pushed his hands off and slid off the counter. I lifted his head and kissed him on the cheek. "Go. Spend the rest of the day with the boys. I've stuff to do today. We will talk later."

He looked worried. "OK. Let's talk later."

I watched him walk out the door. I walked into my room. I grabbed the first cushion I could see and screamed furiously into it. The one thing I hate more than anything is my character being judged. I have worked hard coming to terms with the fact that I am different to other people. I don't like being put into a category. I have a good heart. Why can't people see that?

I spent the remainder of the day cleaning the apartment and unpacking properly. I organised my closet, put on a load of washing and decided to try out the pool on the roof. I needed to clear my head. Why not make use of it?

I stayed out until the sun went down, swimming and relaxing on the sun loungers. I had a shower, put on my pj's and threw myself on the couch. I hadn't responded to any of Yungrae's texts. I just needed to re-evaluate things. I was also petrified of how I was feeling. Everything I have been programmed to know about love and relationships was being contradicted by how much I wanted to be with someone I had just met.

I completely understand if you're reading this and thinking, 'Why the fuck are you two both so intense, when you only met a few days ago?' Believe me, I was asking myself the same thing. Was this not super-weird?. You have to understand, everything felt so right around him. Like I knew him in another life or something. I don't want to use the word soulmate (because, cringe), but I didn't like being apart from him. I knew that if I felt this strongly already, his magnetic pull on me was only going to get more intense as time went on. Was I ready for that?

I needed advice. I immediately checked the time in New York. It was 2.20 p.m. I texted Molly. 'Hey Mol. Are you free? I really need a chat. My head is fried. XX'

Not even two minutes passed and my phone was ringing. "Hey, my love. How are you feeling?"

"Hey, Mols! Ah, not great. I really miss you guys. I need your advice. I want to include Olivia too, but with the time difference, it's hard to get us all together."

"I'll text her, hang on. Its 8.25 a.m. there. She could be awake," Molly said.

"I hope she is!"

"Yeah, she's cool. Hang up and we will facetime."

My phone rang back almost immediately. I needed to tell them in a certain way that didn't give away the surprise. Molly will die when she sees the boys. Olivia was bathed in sweat from the bickrem yoga class she had walked out of when she received Molly's red alert. Molly was walking along the beach in the Hamptons where she had gone to spend time with her father. He had invited her to their summer house and then coincidentally left her alone a day later. She was making the most of the guilt money he had placed on the dining room table along with a note that read 'I'm sorry. Work emergency'. I felt bad for her. I know how much she longs for her father's attention.

"Right, Ami, what's going on? We are here. You have our undivided attention. By the way, where are you?"

I changed to the back camera and showed the girls the living room. I wanted to talk to Molly about how she was feeling but as usual she shut both Olivia and I down the minute we tried to get her to open up. "Girls, It's fine. I'm fine. I'm well used to this by now" she said, smiling unconvincingly. "Now tell me what's been going on with you Ami or I'm hanging up" I reluctantly explained all about my parents, my ex and the apartment.

"Ami. That's crazy, but don't worry, we will be there soon enough to help you decide," Olivia said.

"Oh, yes, well, that brings me to the next spanner in the works." I told them how I had met someone and how last night and this morning went.

They squealed like little girls. I could feel their excitement through the phone.

"Honestly, this news makes me so happy. Where is he from?" Molly asked.

"Ummmm. Well, he's from England, but his parents are Korean." I lied so badly.

"Amelia, this is scary. We are moving to Korea. What are the chances? Is he hot?"

"Oh, you have no idea, girls. He is so sexy. He's so tall, and his voice is so deep. But he has the cutest gummy smile that makes me so happy."

Molly chimed in. "Ami, I can't wait to meet him! Are his friends hot, too?"

"Yes! Extremely handsome and really good fun."

"Oh, yay! I'm so excited. My advice, and I think Molly will agree with me: just relax and stop overthinking this! It sounds very intense, yes, and I understand you're worried that if you allow yourself to get emotionally invested, that you may get hurt. But not everyone is going to disappoint you. You have to start trusting people. They might surprise you."

"Olivia is right, hun! And worst case scenario: he's a dick and you never have to see him again. You're moving halfway across the world. It couldn't be more perfect. A nice summer fling. Just have fun. Enjoy yourself."

I couldn't tell her that he was, in fact, Korean, and a member of the most famous Korean boy band in the world. They were right. I just had to go with it and stop overthinking it.

"Why don't you spend a few days away and see if absence makes the heart grow fonder. Make him miss you a little."

"Yeah, good idea. I might spend time with my sister and the kids. But I'll keep in contact with him, right?"

"Yeah, obviously, Ami. Otherwise he will think you're ghosting him," Molly laughed.

"Now that we've sorted my dilemma, go and enjoy your time with your families. Thanks for everything, girls. I can't even make it a week without you. Love you guys."

We said our goodbyes, and I instantly felt better. I went to get a bottle of water from the fridge, and when I returned, my phone was buzzing again. It was Yungrae. I better stop avoiding him over something silly.

"Hey."

"Hey, Amelia, thank god you're alive. I was seriously starting to worry. Why haven't you texted me back?"

"Sorry, I just needed a few hours to myself. I'm better now! How are you?"

"I'm good, now that I hear your voice. What are you doing?"

"I'm just lying down on the couch. Thinking of going to bed in a minute. I'm so tired. What are you doing?"

"I'm in bed. I have to be up early, we are going to get a boat to San Remo tomorrow. We will spend one night there, so I won't be able to see you. Is that OK?"

"Of course. You should go and have fun with your friends. You're on vacation. I wanted to spend some time with my family, so I won't be around anyway."

"Oh, that's great. Say hello to your sister and her husband for me. We went shopping earlier. I am really tired. Junseo loves spending money. They kept teasing me because I was constantly talking about you." He laughed.

"Sounds like you had fun. I'm glad. Nice is a really cool city. It's great to explore it. I want to let you sleep now. You sound exhausted. I'll text you tomorrow. Goodnight, Yungrae."

"Goodnight, Amelia. Sleep well."

The conversation went way better than I thought. Not awkward at all. I peeled myself off the couch and headed for my bedroom. I was so tired.

Just as I was brushing my teeth, I got a text from Yungrae. 'Are you sure you will text me tomorrow?'

I replied: 'Yes. Goodnight, Yungrae.'

My phone buzzed in a matter of seconds. 'Just checking. Goodnight, beautiful.'

I caught myself smiling in the mirror. "This isn't so bad," I said to myself. I took my happy arse to bed and was sound asleep before I knew it.

Chapter 8

I had spent the last two days with my family. It was very confusing, if I was honest. I had to compartmentalise my feelings just to get through the two days without crying or completely flipping out at my parents. I spent a lot of time in the stables, and in the cool of the evenings, I took one of the horses out for a ride through the vineyard.

My parents cooked such amazing food. I painted with Ali and Ben out in the garden. We took loads of photos on Dad's vintage polaroid camera. I kept some to bring to Seoul with me. David showed me his 'spin off business' that he was starting. He was starting to produce cider and was bringing apples in from Ireland. I tasted a few samples and almost got drunk from the fumes alone. When I was able to relax, it was nice.

I went back to the apartment late that night and pretty much went straight to sleep. I loved the feeling of waking up in my own bed again. I was looking forward to a day to myself. Yungrae arrived back late too, but I wasn't going to see him until the next day. We texted a lot while he was away. He didn't know, but I was planning on taking him to dinner tomorrow night. A night of romance was needed.

I had a hair appointment booked and an outfit picked already.

I got up and ate breakfast in front of the TV. I loved watching the French news. The language is so beautiful. After an hour of lazing around, I got changed into my running gear, with my swimming costume underneath, and headed off. It was extremely warm, and I could have died from dehydration, but I needed to burn off some calories from all the good food I'd been devouring. The sun was so hot, but I persisted with a gentle jog along the 'Promenade des Anglais'. The light breeze helped cool me off slightly. Although I only ran four kilometres, it felt like ten, due to the heat. I must get up earlier when I want to go running.

I was desperately trying to get my breath back to normal, walking to the car to grab my towel and water. I wandered down to the beach, lost in my own inner ramblings. I found a spot on the beach near two old ladies. I knew they would spend their time watching people, so my stuff would be safe. I smiled at them and said hello. They were very friendly and admired my blonde hair. They asked why a pretty girl like me was on my own. I explained I was just out jogging, trying to burn off the wine from last night. They laughed and laughed. They offered me some water, and we chatted a little bit about the weather. They told me they were widows and best friends. It was fun practicing my French again. I was rusty at the start, but it came back to me soon enough. I was explaining how much I loved the sea here and how I missed it so much when I was away. They encouraged me to go in and said they would mind my things. So I jumped up and ripped off my top and shorts.

As I was undressing, I felt like someone was watching me. I brushed it off as paranoia. I'm still quite self-conscious about my body. Even more so in France, where everyone has beautifully bronzed skin and amazing figures. I didn't look the same as I used to. I was healthy and I'd worked hard to lose the weight. Being so pale that I was almost see-through wasn't a bad thing. Someday, if I kept telling myself that enough, I just might believe it.

I walked into the water until it was deep enough to dive under. It felt amazing. I swam for a while. I loved just floating. Looking up at the sky and the hot sun beating down on the parts of my body not under water, was invigorating. I closed my eyes and relaxed.

All of a sudden I felt myself bang into something. Panicked, I stood up to the only thing that could make this day the worst day off my life. There he was. Satan himself. Swimming in the sea.

"Watch where you're going, woman! You're not the only person in the water."

I started to burn up from the inside.

His face changed, and he began smiling at me. "Pugsley? Is that you? Awwwh! You've lost your baby fat. About time." He tried to squeeze my cheeks, but I swatted his hand away.

May I introduce my ex-boyfriend, ladies and gentlemen. A sandy-haired, six-foot-two, muscular demon. I used to be a total pushover and I wouldn't have been able to stand up for myself, but I'd changed a lot over the last year. I'd imagined running into him so many times. I had to remain calm. I couldn't let my emotions get the better of me. Not this time.

"So sorry about that. I wasn't expecting to bump into any rude, condescending pricks. The water is quite cold today, huh? You seem a little shrivelled." I glanced towards his crotch.

He laughed nervously and placed his hands over himself. "Look who's being a cheeky bitch."

I turned to leave the water.

"*Amelia, wait!*" he screamed after me.

I kept walking, with my fists clenched. I was almost at my towel when he grabbed me from behind, pulling me into him. "Your ass looks so much better now that you're no longer colossal," he whispered in my ear.

I pushed my hips back till he released me, and I slapped him across the face. He held his hand to his cheek. I kept walking.

"What the fuck was that for? You stupid bitch. I was being friendly."

I gathered my things. The two old ladies, Sylvie and Brigitte, whom I met earlier, asked me if I was all right. I thanked them, apologised and said goodbye in passing, then stormed off, throwing on my beach dress as I went. He followed me all the way up the beach and continued behind me towards the apartment building.

"Amelia, wait, for fuck's sake. I'm trying to speak to you. How dare you hit me and walk away, with no consequences. You stupid girl. Somethings never change. You're too afraid to speak to me!" he screamed at me.

This made me stop in my tracks. I turned around to face my tormentor. "Fuck you!" I spat.

He grabbed me by my shoulders. "You're enjoying this, aren't you! You little slut! It's like forcplay to you!"

I shoved him away from me with force.

"Hey! Amelia, are you OK?"

I heard someone shout from a distance, but I was too worked up to acknowledge them. "What the fuck did you just say to me? Enjoying this? Are you fucking out of your mind? I want nothing to do with you. You're still a total dickhead. Please fuck off and leave me alone."

He grabbed me again by my shoulders and began shaking me. "Listen, you stupid bitch! You're the one telling your retarded mother that you want to talk and work things out. I'm only doing what I am asked. Your father was stupid enough to promise me fifty percent of the business. All I have to do is marry you and I get everything I have spent the last few years working for. Why do you think I keep playing tennis with him? Why do you think I put up with his stupid jokes? Don't even get me started! All I had to do is get back on your good side, and thankfully you're not half as disgusting as before. You love this. You're telling your mommy how badly you want me back. You're so pathetic. I told you, you would regret ending things!"

He was drooling as he spoke, like a rabid dog. I pushed him from me and tried to get away.

He grabbed me again, this time by my throat. "You'll always be my weak little Pugsley!"

Suddenly I heard someone scream, "Let fucking go of her!"

He pressed me against a car. Tightening his grip on my throat, he said, "I can still take what I want from you, you worthless piece of shit." He spat into my face.

I closed my eyes, afraid of what would happen next. He kept tightening his grip. I was struggling to breathe.

"I said, let her go! Are you deaf or just completely stupid?"

I opened my eyes and saw Yungrae pull him away from me.

"Who the fuck are you?" Richard snapped at Yungrae.

"I'm her boyfriend. Keep your fucking hands off her, or you'll answer to me." Yungrae had a dark expression on his face. He stood glaring at Richard with his fists clenched.

Richard laughed sarcastically. "*Wow*, Pugsley. I can't believe you've really degraded yourself like this. You brought back a yellow, slanty-eyed freak with you. You know he's only with you for a visa, right? You're so desperate." He laughed.

That was enough to tip me over the edge. I swung for him. This time, all the hurt and anger I had been trying to bury for so long came right to the surface. I remembered all the times he had hurt me and made me feel guilty for what he had done. I hit him right between his eyes. The sound of my fist hitting his head was like lightning cracking in the sky.

"Amelia! What the fuck! Why do you keep hitting me?"

I swung again, hitting the other side of his face. "That's for me!" I swung for him again. "That's for being a racist pig! And this one is for using my parents!" I hit him again before he could respond.

He went down on the ground, covering his head with his hands.

Yungrae wrapped his arms around me. "*Enough.* Don't waste any more of your energy. He's not worth it." He pulled me into his chest. I could feel the tears welling up in my eyes. "Hold back those tears if you can. Don't cry in front of him."

He lead me past the group of boys and into the building.

"You'll regret this, you stupid whore!" Richard called out after us.

"OK. He can't see you now. It's safe." He sat me down on the couch in the reception area and knelt in front of me. "Are you OK? Did he hurt you? I will kill him. What kind of an animal would put his hands on a woman? I'm so glad I was there. Are you hurt anywhere?" He pushed the hair out of my face.

"I'm fine. I just feel stupid. I shouldn't have behaved like that. It's just I had a lot of built-up anger, and it got the better of me."

He examined my knuckles.

"Ouch." I pulled my hands away.

"You're going to be bruised." Yungrae asked the guys to get something cold to put on my knuckles. Junseo went over to the vending machine and got three cold cans of coke.

"Why three? I only have two hands," I laughed.

"One is for you to drink. The sugar will help you feel better."

I sipped it in silence. I had finally stood up to him. I know I shouldn't have hit him, but he had hit me enough in the past. I had finally stood up to my bully. I couldn't believe he thought I wanted him back. And my father had promised him shares if we got married? Surely that was a lie. I knew they were close, but come on. How was I going to tell them? They wouldn't believe me. Our relationship was rocky at the best of times, but this could be the final nail in the coffin. He couldn't win this time. I started full-on sobbing. The boys looked shocked.

"Amelia, it's OK. You're safe now. He can't hurt you anymore!" Yungrae hugged me.

"It's not me I'm worried about. It's my family. I shouldn't have touched him. He could use this to weasel his way into my father's company. My dad won't want this to become public knowledge, and Richard knows that! He's going to somehow use it as leverage. I know him too well. He preys on your vulnerabilities."

"Doesn't the building have security cameras? Would that not be evidence against him?" Yungrae asked.

"There's no sound. My dad won't believe me."

Just then, Daeshim piped up. "I have it all on video."

We all turned to face him. "What?"

"I was taking a selfie when we heard the commotion. We saw it was you in trouble, and I knew Yungrae couldn't not get involved, so I started recording in case he beat the shit out of that guy. Turns out you did. You sure can throw a punch. I'm impress…"

I cut him off. "Can you hear everything clearly?"

He nodded and passed me his phone. "Take a look."

Watching it back made me cringe. I was an actual lunatic. I looked crazy. It was hard seeing myself so angry, but the silver lining of the situation was the audio of the video being clearer than the sky was that day. I actually had proof of what a horrible bully Richard was.

"Ohhhhhh," the boys said collectively. "You're a feisty one."

"Man, you knocked that guy clean out!" Jiseok went to high-five me.

"Please don't do that. I am an animal. I am as bad as him. I shouldn't have behaved that way. I want to be someone's wife one day. Who would want to marry me now?" I lowered my head and sobbed again.

Yungrae sat beside me and put his arm around my shoulder. "Please don't say that. He had you pinned to a car with his hands on your neck. I get the feeling that wasn't the only time he's done that. It was self-defence. You were just protecting yourself and your parents. You stood up to a bully. I would have done that and worse to that bastard. When I saw you trying to get away from him,

I saw red. You were in trouble, and I wanted to get to you as fast as I could."

"He was so horrible to you. I'm so sorry. You shouldn't have been spoken to like that."

"Amelia, have you been on Twitter? We've been called much worse." Junseo laughed.

I laughed too. It made me feel better. "This has definitely ruined your day, guys. I'm sorry."

"Stop apologising. None of this is your fault. Let's think how you should show this to your parents," Daeshim chimed in.

I sent the video to my phone and then immediately to my sister. She would know what to do. I lay back in the chair and sighed. All we needed to do now was wait.

My phone rang. "Hello! Ami! I'm going to kick seven kinds of shit out of that guy as soon as I see him. I can't even imagine what David is going to do to him. Or Dad. He's basically just dug his own grave. Are you OK? Did you break your hand? You hit him so hard. Your hand must be shattered. He got off lightly. Also, Yungrae came to the rescue. Ohhhhhh... did I mention I love him? He's husband material."

Yungrae was beaming at me.

I pulled myself and the phone further away from him, afraid of what else she would say. "Oh, Andy, please shut up for a second. My head is spinning. What do I do next? I'm worried sick."

"Well, David's on the phone to the building security team to get the footage from the outside cameras. They will email them straight to me. He's telling the truth about Dad giving him shares — there's been papers drawn up. We just have to get to them first. I have a plan, but I need to drop the kids by you for a while. Is that OK?"

"Of course, but what are you planning? Can I help? It's my fault he was even in our lives."

"Relax, and enjoy your evening with the twins. You have been through enough, clearly. Leave the rest to your big sister. I am here to protect you. It's my job."

"OK. If you're sure. I'm going to wash up and get ready. I'll take them somewhere, for a drive. What time will you be here?"

"I'll drop them by you in about thirty minutes. I hope you're OK. I love you."

"Love you too. See you soon."

"Well, what did she say after you moved so I couldn't hear any more?"

"She's taking care of it, and I'm minding the kids for the evening. I'm going to take them somewhere."

"Cool. Let's both go get ready," Yungrae said, which took me by total surprise.

Before I had a chance to answer, Jiseok pipped up, "Amelia, would it be OK if Taehwan and I came too? The others are going fishing, and it's boring."

"Yeah, would you mind if we tagged along? I'm not a fan of open water, and it draws too much attention when we are all together," Taehwan added shyly.

"Wait, you want to hang out with me and my eight-year-old niece and nephew?"

"We love kids, and we hate fishing. Plus, we kind of want to make sure you're OK. I have a younger sister, and if someone did that to her, I wouldn't know what to do," Taehwan admitted.

"All right, OK. I'm really sorry about earlier, everyone. Enjoy fishing, boys. And you three, let's meet back here in a half hour."

How the hell was I supposed to entertain two eight-year-olds and three twenty-something-year-old boys? Maybe a trip to Eze? Yeah, I hadn't been in years.

I tried to focus on getting ready. I picked out a green, floral playsuit, gold, hoop earrings, my oversized, Balenciaga denim jacket and white Gucci Ace sneakers. My hair had dried funny, so I quickly pulled it up into a high ponytail. I slapped on some makeup and finished with my favourite MAC nude lipstick faux, which I threw into my Prada backpack. I can imagine at this point you are wondering why this was important. I know I shouldn't have cared what I looked like, but it was the only thing I could control in that moment. This wasn't my first time being hurt and I went into my version of survival mode which of course meant carrying on as normal and dealing with what had just happened later. My mind was racing, and my anxiety kicked into overdrive. The funny thing was that I was actually more worried about my family and their reputation than I was about myself. I knew I would be fine eventually. I looked at my reflection in the mirrors in the elevator. I was caressing my throat. It would surely bruise.

It took me five minutes to realise I hadn't pressed the button. I could hear Alison and Ben roaring with laughter, on my way down. I was excited to see them. The elevator doors opened, and the two of them jumped from either side.

"Fucking hell, guys. You scared the life out of me. Oh, ah, sorry. 'Freaking hell', guys."

"Don't worry, they have been exposed to much worse. Have you met their mother?" David reassured me with a smile.

"Auntie Ami, why didn't you tell us you knew 'Neon Embers'? I am a huge fan, you know. Taehwan is my bias, but don't tell him that!" She took my hand and we walked to the boys who were waiting patiently in their seats.

Yungrae got up and kissed me on the cheek. "You look stunning. Especially for an MMA fighter," he whispered in my ear.

I shot him a dirty look.

"Too soon?"

"Yeah. Too soon. I see you've met my wonderful nephew and niece!"

He mouthed, 'I'm so sorry', while Ben gave me a big hug.

"You look lovely. Where are you taking them?" Andrea asked.

"We are going to Eze for the evening. I'm bringing them to the gardens."

"Oh, lovely. You love it there. They have everything in their bag, and they are caked in sunscreen, so don't panic! We have to go. We will see you guys later. We are meeting Mom and Dad."

"Mom, can we stay with Ami tonight? I heard you guys on the phone earlier, and I know someone tried to hurt her. Me and Ben will keep her safe."

Andrea rolled her eyes. "That's up to Amelia, Alison."

I didn't really have the energy to entertain them, but I would pull it from somewhere. "Yeah, of course, if that's OK with you guys?"

The twins gave me two thumbs up.

"All right, but be good. I'll come collect you in the morning. Do as Amelia says." She kissed them both and followed David to the car.

I turned to them. "Right. Well, now that the boss is gone, who's ready to have some real fun?"

"We are, we are! Yay!" they both screamed.

"Let's go. You boys ready?"

"Let's get it!" Taehwan shouted, and we walked to the car.

The two boys sat in the very back, and the twins sat in the middle seat of the car. I was checking my reflection in the mirror when I saw Alison rubbing her lips. "You want some lipstick?"

Her eyes lit up. "Yes, like yours!"

I rummaged through my bag and handed her lipstick and a vanity mirror. "Don't tell your mother! Please!"

She began applying it, and we all started admiring her. Her little giggles warmed my heart.

"Are we all ready now? Yungrae, you're my co-driver today, so you're in charge of the music. My phone is in my bag. Choose wisely." I smiled at him and lowered my Gucci pilot glasses onto my face.

"Yes, ma'am."

I was about to pull out of the car park when Ben asked, "If you're Korean, how can you speak English so well?"

I stopped and turned to face them all.

"Years of strict practice. My pronunciation is the worst. Hello. How are you? I'm fine, thank you, and you?" Taehwan said in a high-pitched voice, in the worst attempt at a British accent that I'd ever heard. "They made us repeat it over and over and over again."

I was so stunned by this sudden outburst that I started to laugh. It must have been contagious, because soon we were all laughing.

"Please. God. Don't do that again!" Yungrae pleaded, before he took my hand and gently kissed my knuckles. "Let's get out of here!" he roared in a similar weird accent, and off we went on our road trip.

Chapter 9

After a fifteen-kilometre drive we arrived in the beautiful village of Eze. The boys were constantly taking pictures the whole time. I found a place to park the car near the entrance to 'Le Jardin exotique d'Eze'. We walked around, looking at all the exotic plants. I loved it so much here. The views are stunning. There's something so peaceful about being around nature like this.

I followed the twins around, showing them different plants and explaining what they were. Yungrae never left my side.

"The three of you can wander off and explore, if you want. I can text you when we are going to the hotel to eat."

"Do you want us to go?" Yungrae looked disappointed.

"No, not at all, but just don't feel you have to be stuck with me and the kids."

"I like being with you, and I like the twins very much. They are good children. Very well-mannered." I wouldn't describe the twins as well-mannered. Quite the opposite really. Especially when I was in change. The only hope I ever had at controlling them was through bribery and it worked for the most part. Hearing him compliment them made me smile.

"I just didn't think this was the type of boy's holiday you guys were on."

Taehwan and Jiseok had come up behind me while I was talking. "We are having an amazing time, Amelia. This place is so beautiful. We wouldn't have seen this place, only for you. You're our tour guide today."

"OK, but just…"

Yungrae covered my mouth with his hand. "Please don't be stubborn."

I bit him.

"Heeeey. That was uncalled for!" he laughed, shaking his hand in the air. "Are you sure you're mature enough to supervise these kids?"

All four of us burst out laughing.

"Jiseok! Taehwan! Come quick, there's butterflies over here!" Alison shouted.

Both of them went to investigate. Yungrae grabbed my hand and pulled me towards a bench. "Let's sit for a while. The boys can watch them. Well, today was eventful. I am sorry that happened to you, Amelia. I hope you're really OK. That was your ex-boyfriend, right?"

"Yes. I broke up with him last year, right before I left for Japan. I found out he was seeing my friend on the side."

"Wow. That must have been a lot to deal with. I can't imagine how you must have felt."

"Yeah. I guess I had plenty of unresolved anger towards him and the situation. He was very violent towards me, and he did some unspeakable things to me while we were together. I don't know where I mustered up the courage to leave. I guess I knew if I didn't go as far away from him as I could, my life would always be like that."

My face must have shown just how uncomfortable I was, because Yungrae took my hand and said, "Amelia, if you're not up to talking about it, we don't have to. Just know I am here for you, anytime that you do. I think it would do you good to get these things off your chest. You don't have to carry this with you forever. I'll help you in any way that I can."

I was relieved. "It's hard for me to talk about, because I feel so ashamed of myself. I let him continuously hurt me, and he made me feel like I deserved it. My parents adored him, so I thought it was just something wrong with me. My parents never liked any of my boyfriends before him, and it was exhausting trying to fight their opinions. When I met Richard, he was so charming. My parents instantly loved him, and I guess it was just nice to be with someone they approved of. I don't know if any of that makes sense!"

"It does. It makes perfect sense. Of course we want our parents to approve of everything we do in life. My parents didn't want me to follow my dreams, and it killed me to defy them. But it is my life, and sometimes you have to just trust your gut. People can project their fears onto you, and it can make you question everything. You just have to trust your own voice, because only you know what you're truly capable of. My parents felt it would be more beneficial to me to stay home, go to college, get a real degree and become a businessman. I didn't, and look where I am now. Sitting in the most beautiful place with an even more beautiful girl."

I started blushing. He took my chin in his hand. "Some people see beautiful things and want to possess them. Take the flowers in this garden, for instance. Some people will see a pretty flower and think, 'Yeah I want that,' so they pick it. They pull it from the soil, damaging it. It only lasts awhile without proper nourishment before it wilts and dies. Other people see a flower and fall in love with it. They think they have never seen anything like it before, until they go to another garden and see a different flower and they forget all about the first one. But one person may see this beauty and want to know everything about it: what soil it grows best in; what kind of sustenance it needs; how often to water it or how much sunlight it should get. He digs up the plant, carefully gathering all its roots, and takes it home with him and plants it. There the flower is treated with kindness and gets everything it needs, including love. It is appreciated every day for the rest of its life."

I was trying my best to understand what he meant.

"Do you understand?"

"Not really." I shook my head.

"If you're potted in the wrong environment or the wrong soil, you will never grow to your full potential, Amelia. People will always think they know what you need, but only you can feel your roots. Only you know what needs you have under the surface. You know your true heart. Don't let anyone tell you they know what's best, because that might mean you get trampled on or picked up by the wrong gardener."

I smiled at him. "I get what you are saying. That was actually beautifully said. No wonder you're an amazing songwriter." I kissed him on the cheek. "Thank you."

"For what?"

"For staying when you didn't have to. For being here with me now, holding my hand. It means so much to me."

"I'm here because I really want to be. I feel at ease with you. Anyway, you would do the same for me."

"I know I would. I've been waiting for a very long time to find someone to be there for me like I would them." I placed my head on his shoulder and closed my eyes. The world didn't seem so scary. Life didn't always have to be so hard.

"You guys are adorable."

I opened my eyes to Taehwan taking pictures of us. "Really? I must look a mess."

Yungrae immediately snapped the phone out of his hands and examined the pictures. "I want all of them. Send them to me and then delete them." His smile was enough to make me curious.

"Oh for God's sake! Let me see." I was surprised. I looked so happy and relaxed. He was so handsome. Even more so in real life. We sort of fit together like two puzzle pieces. Our bodies slotted together like we were made to make up one whole being. I couldn't help but smile too. "You're actually a good photographer, Taehwan."

"Thank you. I try. You both are good models. It's best to take pictures of people when they are happy. They just glow from the inside." He smiled at me.

Alison and Ben came running back to us, followed by Jiseok. "Look what we found!" She opened her palms to expose the largest spider I have ever seen in real life.

"*Ahhhhhhh*, Jesus, Ali! Keep that thing away from me!" I ran away screaming while they all laughed at me. "It's not funny. Its gross. Drop it now, or I'm leaving you all here."

Alison placed the spider on the ground reluctantly and dusted her hands on her brother's jumper.

"*Alison!*" he screamed at her, and they began bickering.

I walked over as soon as it was safe to do so and began separating the twins. "That's enough, guys. Let's not make a show of ourselves. Who's hungry?"

"We are!" They both shook hands and put their arms around one another. "We'll be good. We promise. Can we get ice cream after dinner?"

"As long as there's no more arguments. Yes. That's fine." I gestured to the boys to come along.

The five of us wandered through the beautiful town of Eze. The narrow streets paved our way to *Château de La Chèvre d'Or*, where we would be eating. We walked into the arch to meet my friend, Marcel, waiting for us. "*Oh bon soirée,* Amelia! *Ça Va?*" He kissed me on either cheek.

"*Ça va très bien, et toi?*"

"Oh, you know me. I am busy, busy, busy. It is so wonderful to see you. Who are those handsome boys, Amelia? Are you collecting them? *Bon soirée à tous.* Come! Come!" He waved us on through the door, taking my hand under his arm. "Amelia, what is going on? I haven't seen you in so long, and you bring three delicious-looking men to see me. Are they a gift?"

I laughed. "It all depends on where you seat us."

"Oh, but of course. Is outside OK? I have the perfect table."

We were seated overlooking the French Rivera. Alison wouldn't sit down — she was looking around, taking it all in.

"Alison, are you going to join us?" I asked.

"Is this really the place?" She sat down. She seemed almost star-struck.

"What do you mean, Al?"

"The place you wanted to get married? I remember Mom showed me pictures. You guys first came here when you were my age, right?"

I suddenly remembered why this place meant so much to me. "I can't believe I forgot. Of course. I made your Mom write it in her scrapbook. Yes, this is where I said I wanted to have my wedding." I was blushing so hard.

Yungrae's eyes were glued to me. "I didn't realize you were such a romantic, Amelia! This place is idyllic."

"Yeah, it's beautiful here, and the food's amazing. The garden is all lit up at night, and the sea behind you... It's just perfect." I kept avoiding eye contact.

He placed his hand on mine. "Well, maybe one day. After you grow in the right soil." He winked at me.

The time flew by. We were fed and watered and heading back to the car.

As we were fastening our seat belts, Jiseok popped his head between the seats. "Amelia, who was the guy at the restaurant? He kept winking at me. Do you think he was... I don't know... hitting on me?"

I couldn't help but smile at his innocence. "That's Marcel. He's friends with my friend, Madelyn. And yes, he was most definitely hitting on you!"

"I was wondering when he asked for my number on the way to the bathroom. I told him we were at table three and that he should know; he sat us there!"

We all burst into laughter.

"How does that make you feel, Jiseok?" Taehwan asked.

"Great. It's nice that he, too, appreciates my handsome face." He joined us in laughing.

The drive home was nice. We all chatted about things we saw. I promised the twins we would get ice cream, so we stopped near the apartment for a treat. We sat outside the ice cream parlour while the sun began setting. It was the perfect way to end the day that had started so horribly. I was in such a good mood. Nothing could ruin this.

"Our bedtime is nine thirty, now, Auntie. So we have time to watch a movie when we get back."

"You know, guys, I was thinking about that. I think that since it's rare that we get to have sleepovers, that maybe we just go to sleep when we feel tired?"

"So no bedtime?" Ben shouted.

"No bedtime. Instead of staying inside, I was thinking we go up to the roof for a swim? I have loads of new floaties that I haven't used yet."

"Yeeeessss!" The twins high-fived. "This is the best night ever."

"You guys are more than welcome to join us!"

Taehwan and Jiseok looked at each other. "Pool party!" they shouted in unison.

Alison and Ben were squealing in delight. When we arrived at the apartment, the boys went to get ready for swimming and to see if the others wanted to join. I began searching for swimsuits in the twins' overnight bag. The three of us got ready and headed for the roof.

The twins immediately dived into the water, so I took the opportunity to call my sister. "Hey, Andy, how are things now?"

"Hey, love. I told you not to worry. I thought you'd be too distracted by the terrible twosome to even think about calling me."

"Stop calling them that! They are your kids, and they are so well-behaved. What happened?"

"Well, I started off explaining the situation to them, and of course, they were in disbelief. I showed them the video and the CCTV footage from the front of the building. Mom cried. Dad smashed a glass. Then Dad ripped up and then burnt any documents he had drawn up. Now he's on the phone to his lawyers to see if there's a way to get away with murder."

"What?" The blood drained from my face.

"Relax, I'm kidding. He is on to them, but he is just trying to figure out which way is best to go about dealing with this. They are hoping that you will forgive them and sit down for a discussion about it soon."

"OK, well, I'm not really ready to talk about it yet, Andy. I don't even know how to process this. I have been a victim of this guy for far too long. I think I will start seeing my therapist again. Maybe it will help."

"Again? Amelia, when were you seeing a therapist?" She sounded upset.

I started wandering around the edge of the water while we spoke. "In Japan. I sort of needed it after I left. I was struggling a little. I wasn't there too long, and I began having panic attacks, so Molly and Olivia helped me find someone to talk to. She put me on a course of anti-anxiety meds that really transformed me. I promise I am doing so much better, but it would be no harm to check in with her."

"Amelia. I don't know what to say to you. I wished you had told me. I would have been on the first flight out."

"It's OK. Really, Andrea. I wasn't alone. It really helped me. I'm OK now. Let's talk about it some other time. I'm tired."

"OK, we will talk about it, though. Ami, why is there screaming in the background? What are those two up to?"

"Ah, well, we are currently swimming. I hope that's OK. We were having such a nice afternoon, I wanted it to end on a high!"

"Amelia. As long as they are breathing and still have all their teeth, I don't care what you guys do. I don't need to know. Just enjoy your time with them. They really missed you while you were away."

"I missed them too. OK, let me get back to being the fun auntie. Thank you for everything. I love you so much."

"I love you too, kiddo. I'll talk to you in the morning. I'll pick them up around ten."

No sooner had I hung up the phone, than a text arrived from Yungrae: 'The beach boys are here.'

I ran down to let them into the apartment.

"We bought beers and Junseo and Daeshim." Yungrae greeted me with a kiss on the cheek.

The five boys and I headed up to the roof where the twins were practicing diving.

"You look incredible in that swimsuit. You need to wear them more often," Yungrae whispered in my ear, placing his hand on the small of my back.

My back tingled from the feel of his hand on my skin, and the feeling radiated throughout my entire body. My cheeks were on fire. He laughed at me and placed his things on a sun lounger.

"Who wants a beer?" Jiseok offered.

All five adults' hands shot up. Jiseok handed me one first. "You deserve this after the day you've had."

"Thanks. I doubt it would be strong enough to ease my feelings about today."

"Well, I'm glad you said that, because…" He began rummaging in his bag and pulled out three green bottles. "…I bought soju. Have you any shot glasses?" He broke into the biggest smile.

I wandered into the bar area and got six glasses. They began giving me lessons on drinking in Korea. I wasn't to pour my own drink. I had to turn to the side when drinking in front of elders.

The night grew darker, and the twins were really taking the diving seriously, so we decided to have a competition. Taehwan would be the judge. We took turns jumping in and out of the water. Hours must have passed, and the cans and bottles began building up. Yungrae and I didn't drink much. I wanted to stay as sober as possible. I was glad I didn't, because at 10.12 p.m., a figure appeared at the top of the pool, shouting at me to get out. It was my mother. *Here comes the drama.*

I wrapped up in my towel and followed her downstairs. I knew I was in for a bollocking.

"What in god's name is going on here, Amelia? I come here feeling desperately sorry for you, thinking you would be in bits, only to find you partying with five strange boys, and my grandchildren in the middle of it. Did you ply them with alcohol? It's worse that you're getting. How can you still be so immature! Your sister left those kids in your care, and this is what you get up to? And who are those boys? Where did you pick them up? I don't understand why you can't stick to your own race!" She slapped me across my face.

My mouth fell open. Tears welled up in my eyes. "Once again, you jumped to ridiculous conclusions. Firstly, I have had the same can of beer for the past hour and a half. I would never get drunk while I'm minding my nephew and niece. Andrea knew I was allowing them to stay up late and go swimming. I was on the phone to her. Secondly, those strange boys are the people that were there for me today. One of them is actually the guy I am seeing. If not for him, I would have been strangled outside the front of this building. I'm very sorry that he doesn't suit your newfound racist beliefs and that you would much prefer me to be with someone who constantly abuses me physically and mentally. I am truly sorry to disappoint you. Thirdly, don't ever lay a finger on me again! Now, I would appreciate it if you would fuck off out of this apartment. I am going back upstairs to hang out with my nephew and niece, and my friends who happen to be Korean. If Andrea wants to come for the kids, she knows where they are! I presume you know where the door is?" I stormed off, meeting Alison hiding on the stairs. I bent down to be in her eyeline. "Were you eavesdropping, little one? That's not good, you know."

"I was worried we got you into trouble. I want to talk to Nana before she goes." She pushed past me and ran towards where I left my mother, who was still standing there. "Nana, I love you, but you were too mean to my Auntie. Yungrae, Jiseok, Taehwan, Junseo and Daeshim are my friends too, so if you want to slap me too, go ahead. I like having fun with them. Yungrae makes Auntie Ami smile and laugh. I like him. You have made me angry, Nana. I don't think you were very nice. Me and Ben don't want to go home with you, so you must leave. I will see you on Sunday. I hope you will be nice again." She turned on her heals and came back to hug me.

My mother stood in shock after being called out by a child. We walked hand in hand back to the pool party. We must have stayed up there for another hour before the twins started yawning and rubbing their eyes.

"Right, kids, let's get showered and go to sleep. You both must be exhausted."

"We will go, also. It has been a long day." Junseo, Jiseok, Taehwan and Daeshim began gathering their things.

"I'll clean up here. You get Ben and Alison ready for bed. I'll come in to say goodbye when I'm done," Yungrae said.

It took exactly thirty minutes to shower, brush their teeth and get them into their pyjamas. I plaited Alison's hair, and she jumped into bed beside her brother.

"We had a really good day, Ami. We love you so much. Goodnight!"

I kissed them both and turned off the light. I wondered if Yungrae was still here. I eventually found him in the kitchen, staring at an unopened bottle of red wine. "Are you OK?"

He jumped when he saw me. "You frightened me, Amelia." He held his hand over his chest. "I was debating on whether or not I should open this and have a glass with you, but to be honest, I'm exhausted."

I walked over and hugged his back. "It's fine. I'm so tired after today. I just want to climb into bed."

He turned around to face me and pulled me into his chest. "You had a hard day today. I hope your mother wasn't too mad at you. I hope you will sort things out."

"I'm fine. It's nothing I haven't dealt with before. I'm tough when I have to be, you know."

"Amelia, you're stronger than anyone I know, but you don't have to take the world on by yourself. I'm here for you."

A tiny voice in my head was screaming not to trust him, but I decided to ignore it. "I'm starting to see that. Thank you for today. It means a lot. You should go now. I need plenty of beauty sleep for our date tomorrow."

He backed away slightly to look at me. "We are still going ahead with that? Are you sure you're up to it?" he asked, concerned.

"Of course. I have to plant myself in the right soil, remember?"

He smiled and cupped my face to kiss me repeatedly. The feeling lingered on my lips after we said our goodbyes, and I made my way into bed. His kisses were like a lullaby I wished I could fall asleep to. I pulled the duvet up to my chin and fell asleep to the thought of hearing this melody again tomorrow.

Chapter 10

I woke up to the sound of the doorbell. I had tossed and turned for most of the night. My anxiety was in overdrive after yesterday's dramatic turn of events.

I stumbled up the hallway to the front door, like a caveman who had just learned how to walk. I caught a glimpse of myself in the hall mirror. My hair stood from every direction possible, making me look like I had been dragged through a hedge backwards. All I could do was laugh. Yungrae was one lucky man. Luckily he didn't stay over and wake up next to me this morning.

I opened the door to find the biggest bunch of dark-red roses. I almost smothered myself smelling them. I was smiling wider than a Cheshire cat. I noticed the card attached.

'There are darkness's in life, and there are lights,
And you
are one of those lights,
The light of all lights.'
I turned the card over.
'See you tonight, beautiful — Yungrae.'

I couldn't believe that the first bunch of flowers I had ever received from a guy, came with a quote by Bram

Stoker. My heart could have burst. I took the flowers to the kitchen and began my search for a vase. There had to be one here somewhere. I rooted around in the cupboards until I found what I was looking for. I then prepped and placed the flowers inside their new home and filled it with water. Now all I had to do was decide where to show them off. I fussed over locations around the apartment until I placed them on the glass table in the hallway. Perfect. I stuck my face into them for the thousandth time and drank in their rosy aroma. I loved the smell of fresh flowers almost as much as I loved receiving them. It had definitely made up for the terrible night's sleep I had had.

The doorbell rang again and was followed by constant knocking. Who the hell was that aggressive first thing in the morning? I made eye contact with myself in the mirror. The purple shadows under my eyes and lack of colour on my cheeks made me look like I had woken from a seven-year coma. The bruised ring at the base of my throat stuck out like a sore thumb. My skin glistened with natural oils that had drawn itself to the surface overnight, and I still hadn't brushed my teeth. This was not the version of myself I wanted the person at the other side of the door to meet.

I scrapped my hair into a high ponytail and wiped my face with my sleeve. *This is as good as it's going to get*, I told myself, before reaching for the door and peering my head around it.

It was Junseo. I breathed a sigh of relief until I saw his expression. My anxiety took over again. "Hey! Is everything OK?"

He pushed the door open, exposing me in my Hello Kitty pyjamas. "You just got up, huh? I need to talk to you. Can I come in?" He came in past me before I had a chance to answer.

"Yeah! Sure! Make yourself at home!" I said sarcastically.

"Where can we speak privately?"

"You're starting to really worry me. Is everything OK?" I asked, this time really stressing my words.

"Yeah. I just want to talk to you about yesterday. Yungrae has gone shopping with Jiseok and Taehwan this morning. I thought it best that we have a conversation."

"All right, come into the kitchen. I'll put the kettle on!"

"That's a western thing, is it? I seem to be always drinking coffee here," he laughed.

"It's an Irish thing, and you're lucky it's the morning. Otherwise we'd be drinking alcohol."

"Hey, just so you know, I'm cool with either."

I had only just noticed the iPad under his arm, but I kept talking to try and hide my nerves. "Have you eaten breakfast? Do you want me to make you something?"

"No, I'm fine, thank you. I'm here to talk about you and what happened yester…"

I cut him off midsentence. "Just a coffee for you? Or would you prefer tea? There is cereal here and fresh orange juice. Would you like a glass? I can make you an omelette or something, if you want. Maybe some scrambled eggs and bacon?"

"*Amelia!* Coffee is perfect! Stop trying to distract me with food!"

"Why? Was it working?" I smiled sweetly at him.

He shook his head without breaking his serious face.

"OK, fine. What do you need to say to me that is so important?" I handed him the mug of coffee and sat beside him at the kitchen table.

"Well, first off, I just want to say I hope you're OK after yesterday. That was awfully upsetting to watch. You seem like a sweet girl, and that is why I feel obligated to talk to you. If what happened yesterday had gotten out to the press, you would be having this conversation with lawyers, managers, public relation teams and that kind of thing. I didn't realize how serious this thing has become between you two. I mean, it's only been a matter of days, but if you two are going to continue on this journey, I feel you should be aware of everything that is at stake. Yungrae doesn't know what it is like to have a relationship be revealed to the world. I do, so I'm going to do whatever I can to help you guys. Just as long as you are prepared for the backlash."

"Backlash? What do you mean... backlash? Why would there be backlash?" My stomach dropped.

"Well, Amelia, firstly, you need to be prepared for every fan in the world wanting to know everything about you. Everything about your family. Every detail of your life and relationships. Now, while many of them will support you both, there is a huge possibility that you will receive a lot of criticism. Some may get very nasty, Amelia."

At this stage I was just staring at the cup in my hands. My heart felt heavy, like someone had pulled the rug right from under me. My facial expression must have given away what I was thinking.

"I'm not telling you this to upset you. Please don't misunderstand my motive. I'm trying to help. I tried to talk to Yungrae about this last night, but he is so caught up in the romance of it all, he wouldn't listen to me. Our fans are truly the greatest thing that we have. They make every hardship we face worth it. But we are also marketed in a way which makes them feel that we physically belong to them. We are marketed as if we are their boyfriends; that our day begins and ends with them. So when someone could potentially take their place in our hearts, it can be hard for them to understand. Some don't see us as human beings that need companionship and a personal life outside of our work. Unfortunately that means that our significant others become targets. They will dig up everything they can on you and expose all the dark things in your past." He pushed the iPad over to me with his head lowered, a pained look on his face. "Look at this, please. You need to know the worst-case scenario."

The presentation contained clips from local and international news groups, Instagram posts, Twitter threads, clips from fan-based YouTube accounts, gossip columns, statements made by the company who managed them, and lastly, a death notice.

"So your girlfriend... took her... own life?" My eyes welled up with tears.

"That is the worst part of all this, Amelia. I only met this girl once. I wasn't careful with my actions around her, and the whole thing was blown out of proportion. That girl felt she could no longer go on living, because of me. Because I appeared to be too friendly with her. If we hadn't met on the set of that music video and those gossip reporters hadn't followed our team that day, she would still be alive. I will never forgive myself for it."

I placed my hand on his and gently squeezed it. "I am so sorry, Junseo, but please know that that was not your fault. Those people who wrote those terrible things are the ones who should be held accountable. She made the decision to end her life; it is not your fault. You couldn't have known that she would do that. I am so sorry that this has happened to you. You are a good person and an amazing friend. You don't need to carry this on your shoulders."

He placed his hand on mine. "That is why I am trying to warn you now, before you end up in a similar situation. No one deserves that type of abuse. Sadly, this is the downside of our job. It is the darkness that forms in the shadows caused by being under a spotlight. I don't want either of you to be hurt like this."

I understood where he was coming from. Could I handle all of that? Could my family? Think of everything

I'd ever posted on social media. Imagine what Richard would do if he knew the damage he could cause us. Was I ready for that? Was I strong enough? Were we strong enough, after only knowing each other for such a short time?

"Thank you for coming to me with this. You have given me a lot to think about. I promise I will do what is best for Yungrae. I only have his best interests at heart. Please know that."

He looked at me, concerned. "There is something else. Last night, the story broke internationally that we are here on vacation. So that means we will be under close watch everywhere we go. We can't just spontaneously meet with you and your friends in public any more. Everything we do will have to be planned in advance. Security will have to be increased in a major way. We have to take separate taxis everywhere. Most importantly, you cannot be seen with any of us publicly."

I suddenly felt crushed. "I understand." I was trying my best not to cry.

"Amelia, that means whatever you had planned for tonight..."

"I understand. Consider it cancelled. We won't be seeing each other."

"No, I don't mean you can't see each other. I was trying to say that you just have to become a bit more creative."

"Really? You think we should still keep things going under wraps?"

"Look, maybe I've come on a bit too strong with all of this. I don't understand fully what you both mean to one another, especially given that you guys barely know one another. But I have known Yungrae for a very long time, and I've honestly never seen him this happy. I mean, if he's started writing lyrics about it, then it must be something very special."

I looked up at him so fast I almost gave myself whiplash. "What? Lyrics... about me?"

He covered his mouth with his hand briefly. "I think I've said too much. Bro code and all that! Don't tell him I told you. He tries to be cool, but he's really quite soft. He wears a mysterious armour to hide that fact that he is an emotional guy."

He laughed and it made me feel a little better knowing that Yungrae might be as in touch with the emotional side of his brain as I was. Maybe he felt the world as deeply as I did. "Thank you, truly, for your advice, and for sharing your story with me. I appreciate your honesty. You've given me plenty to think about."

I walked with him to the door.

"Whatever you both decide to do, please know we will be behind you both one hundred percent. I will help you in any way that I can! All of us will." He gave my arm a light squeeze before walking out into the corridor.

I closed the door behind him and slid my back against the wall until I slumped onto the cold floor tiles. Junseo's revelations had made my head spin. Should we see each other or not? I wish someone could just tell me straight, instead of giving me options. I didn't like being placed at a crossroads. It reminded me of a poem by Robert Frost that I learned in secondary school:

'Two roads diverged in a yellow wood,
And sorry I could not travel both
And be one traveller, long I stood
And looked down one as far as I could
To where it bent in the undergrowth;
Then took the other, as just as fair,
And having perhaps the better claim
Because it was grassy and wanted wear,
Though as for that the passing there
Had worn them really about the same,
And both that morning equally lay
In leaves no step had trodden black.
Oh, I kept the first for another day!
Yet knowing how way leads on to way,
I doubted if I should ever come back.
I shall be telling this with a sigh
Somewhere ages and ages hence:
Two roads diverged in a wood, and I,
I took the one less travelled by,
And that has made all the difference.'

Should I take the road 'less travelled by', if it led me to Yungrae? Yes. My heart answered for me. My head was still processing. Yes. Both finally agreed. My head and heart told me to at least try. If I chose the easy option, I wouldn't be me. So I went with giving things a chance.

"Ami, what are you doing?" Alison's little head popped around the corner.

"Good morning, gorgeous! Nothing, I'm just taking… a break." I love kids. They never question you when you're doing weird shit.

"Oh, OK, cool. Who brought you these roses? Oh, I bet it was Yungrae. That's so romantic. Is this the card? Can I read it?"

I nodded, and she joined me on the floor.

She read over it for a minute before turning over to read the back. "Oh, it was him. That's so nice. Did you call him yet?"

"No, I didn't get a chance. I left my phone in my room."

"Well, what are you waiting for, lady! Come on! Let's do it! Do you want to put this in your box of special things?" She fiddled with the small envelope in her hands.

"Ah, excuse me, miss! How did you know about that?"

"Mom told me you keep a box with all your special memories in it, and you look at it when you're sad."

"Well, she's right. I look at it any time I am feeling sad or lonely. I only keep really important things in that box, things that will make me feel happy."

"Yungrae makes you happy, Auntie. Your smile is so wide when he is around that I can see all your front teeth."

I couldn't help but laugh. "So you think I should put this in the box?"

"Yes... and I would really like to see what is in it!"

"Me too, Ami! I want to see if we are in it!" Ben appeared out of nowhere.

"How did I end up with such a nosey nephew and niece?" I laughed.

"Just lucky, I guess," Ben said, nonchalantly.

"Come on, then, I'll show you." I lead them into the back of my closet and pulled down the old biscuit tin from the back of the top shelf. I opened it and began pulling all my old memories out, one by one. I had pictures of the day I won my first show jumping competition, old rosettes, my basketball medal, cinema tickets, every aeroplane ticket from every flight I had been on, and pictures of my grandparents, my parents, and my sister and my brother-in-law on their wedding day . I had pictures of the twins, the day they were born and a picture of every birthday they had. There were a few dozen polaroid's of Olivia, Molly and myself during our time in Japan. I had recently added the photos we had taken at home a few days before. Everything important to me was in that box.

"Wow, Ami! This is so cool. I think me and Ben should make one so we can look at it when we miss you! Do you really have to go again soon?"

My heart sank. "Yes. I'm afraid I do, but I'm only a phone call away, and you can come visit anytime you want!"

"That's what you said last time, and we didn't see you for a whole year!" Alison said with a pout.

Tears started building up in my eyes.

"And I don't think Nana will let us go to Korea if she is now racist!" Ben added.

"Nana isn't really racist. She was just angry at me for something silly. It will all be fine soon. Don't worry! How about we make your mom promise to bring you to see me?" I said, trying to swallow the guilt.

They both nodded unenthusiastically.

"We will spend as much time as we can while I am here, and I will help you start your own special boxes, filled with your special memories! That way, when I come home or you come to see me, you can show me everything I missed while I was away. That sound good? Let's start by taking our very first picture for the box!"

I took out my polaroid camera and took three selfies of us. I placed one in my own box and put it back on the shelf. I got two shoe boxes down and emptied them. I gave one to each of them.

They were discussing how they would decorate them before I interrupted. "Now, guys! I don't know about you both, but I'm starving! What's the one thing your mother won't allow you to have for breakfast?"

They both looked at each other before shouting, "Pancakes!"

"Let's make pancakes then!"

The three of us headed for the kitchen. I decided to call Yungrae while I was cooking breakfast.

He answered on the third ring. "Hey beautiful! I was hoping to hear from you sooner! Did you check outside your front door?"

"I did, and I'm sorry I didn't get a chance to call until now! They are so beautiful! Thank you so much. Junseo stopped by just as I put them into a vase. They are perfect in the…"

"Junseo came to see you? Why would he do that? I warned him not to. That's just not fucking cool. Amelia, I'm sorry, I have to go." Just like that, he hung up the phone. He sounded so annoyed.

I decided it was best to text him:

'Hey! Please don't be upset with Junseo. I'm really happy he came to talk to me. I am a stranger to him, and it must have been difficult for him to open up. I would like to talk to you about it soon, maybe not tonight. I don't want to kill the mood. I'm glad Junseo came to me when he did. I have had to rethink our plans for later and make things a little more intimate. So be ready to be swept off your feet. I will text you the details closer to the time. Thinking of you xx'

The angry, sizzling sounds coming from the frying pan pulled me back into reality. "*Shit*! Sorry, you guys. This first one was just a practice pancake. The next one will be perfect. I promise."

The twins were giggling uncontrollably at this stage. I forced myself to concentrate on the task at hand. I was five or six pancakes in when my sister burst into the kitchen.

"Good morning, everyone!" Andrea bellowed from the doorway. "Sorry I'm a little early, Ami. I missed my babies, and my husband was driving me nuts." She rushed over and squeezed the twins.

"It's fine. We are busy making pancakes. Will you join us?"

"Yum. Yes, please. We never have pancakes at home. David doesn't agree with having dessert for breakfast." Andrea rolled her eyes.

After countless pan flips, we sat down to eat. I was dying to know how last night went, but I knew we couldn't discuss it in front of the kids. Although I had a sneaky suspicion that Alison already knew. She was extremely clingy with me.

She must have heard my thoughts because she suddenly blurted out, "Mom? Nana came over last night and screamed at Amelia. She said really mean things about Yungrae! I told her off, though! She was just trying to ruin our diving competition!"

Andrea's mouth fell open. "Mom did *what*? What did she say? Did she scream at you in front of everyone?"

Suddenly my mother's voice entered the room. "No, I screamed at her inside. Alison was spying on us from the steps!" My mother entered the room sheepishly. "I have come to apologise to you, Amelia. I shouldn't have behaved like that or said what I said! I didn't sleep all night, thinking about you."

"OK, I seriously need to change the passcode for the door. You all can't keep bursting in here when you feel like it."

She was carrying flowers in her hand, and a Gucci bag swung from her wrist. She placed both on the kitchen counter and walked towards me. My mother never admits she is wrong, let alone apologises, so I knew this was hard for her. I got up and hugged her. I still had a lot of anger towards her, but I needed to save my energy for now. We could sort the past out another time.

I pulled out of her embrace to see her shocked expression. She must have expected me to put up more of a fight, but honestly, I was so fed up with the battles. Our family war had to come to an end at some point. Someone had to wave the white flag; why shouldn't it be me?

Alison immediately got up and announced that Ben and herself were going to watch TV in the living room. She dragged her clueless brother out of the room by his sleeve, leaving the three of us in silence. We looked at one another as the tension in the room slowly eased. The wall between my mother and I suddenly became like a picket fence dividing gardens. It was like neighbours meeting for the first time. I reached out my hand to greet her. Maybe we could live in harmony, once and for all?

Chapter 11

I don't know how much time had actually passed, but it felt like an eternity and one of us had yet to speak. I was just standing there, holding my mother's hand like a child on their first day of school. Stuck in this moment, I feared that once someone spoke, our little truce would be over.

The silence was starting to become suffocating, so I decided to be the first to speak. "Thanks for coming, Mom. We have much to discuss. I don't want us to be in this position again. I'm tired of fighting." I gestured for her to take a seat.

Andrea jumped up to make coffee for us. I stared at my mother until she eventually responded.

"Yes, Amelia. I agree. I'm tired of fighting. Nobody really wins. We are all we have. I am sorry for how I spoke to you yesterday. I was so frustrated at the whole situation, and I took it out on you. It was wrong of me. I spent the entire night rewatching the footage from yesterday. I can't believe it. Richard had us all fooled. I really thought he was one of the good ones. Obviously, I was very much mistaken. I have this gut-wrenching feeling that wasn't the first time that pig put his hands on you." Tears started flowing down my mother's face.

I wasn't sure she could cry, to be honest, so I was bit taken aback. I knew it was now or never. Time to tell them everything. "No, Mom, it wasn't the first time, but luckily it was only the second time that he physically hurt me, although he was very abusive and controlling. He would freak out at me all the time — if I spoke to any other guys, if I wore too much makeup, or if I spoke back to him. I was too embarrassed to say anything. I thought I deserved it. I used to defend myself as best as I could. I didn't know how to tell anyone I was being bullied by my boyfriend. It seemed stupid to say out loud. Especially since he was the perfect boyfriend in public. The day I broke up with him, he flipped out at me and burst my lip. I got away before anything else happened, and I told you guys that I fell while drunk."

My sister and mother were sobbing at that point.

"Ami, I can't believe you went through that. We have seen how aggressive he can be. Why didn't you tell us any of this?" Andrea howled.

"I honestly didn't think you would believe me over him. I thought he loved me and that he was telling me the truth because he loved me. I kept telling myself that he wasn't being mean; he was being honest. I really wanted a boyfriend, and I felt lucky that someone that looked like him wanted to be with someone like me. You might find it hard to believe, but I thought it was normal. I began telling Maddie about how sometimes when I would wake up after drinking too much the night before, I would be really sore, and I couldn't remember that we had sex. I didn't even think that it was abnormal. One morning I woke up covered in blood, but I specifically remember putting a tampon in before I passed out asleep. My period was early that month, and I hadn't told him. He screamed at me for destroying the sheets and mocked me about it for weeks after. Only for Maddie telling me how fucked up that was, I wouldn't have thought any more about it. Things finally changed when I found out he was sleeping with Evie, my old friend. I realised that he didn't love me like he said. I didn't want to be treated like that ever again.

"Please don't be upset, Mom. I am OK. I promise. I started seeing a therapist in Japan. I started having massive panic attacks and holding my breath in my sleep. Luckily I had Molly and Olivia to help me through it. I went on medication for a little while. It really helped. I've never felt better."

My mother took my hand and kissed it. "I'm so sorry that you didn't have our support. I am sorry you couldn't come to us for help. I'm so proud of you for breaking his hold on you and for bettering yourself. You should never have had to be with someone like that. I will help you in any way I can. Your father and I will do whatever it takes to help you through this. We have your back, Amelia. You will never feel alone again. We love you."

Andrea wrapped her arms around my shoulders. "Things will be better. We promise. We love you so much."

"So what happens with Richard now? Do we press charges or what? I mean, I don't want the drama, but a restraining order against him, for all of us, would be nice."

"Your father is already working on it, my love. Please don't stress. We will handle everything."

"I just want to put this all behind me and move on. I'm so over this. I have had such a good year abroad, and I've met such amazing people. I want to leave all this negativity in the past."

"We all want that for you, Amelia. It's our fault that he was still in our circle, even while you were away. I got you something this morning. Cecile, in the store, said you were looking at these the other day, and I remembered how much you loved Carrie Bradshaw's 'Carrie' necklace in Sex And The City."

She handed me the Gucci bag. Inside was a necklace with the letter 'A' on it. It was beautiful.

"I know it's not your full name, but I wanted you to always have something to remind you of who you are. Our Amelia. Strong, with the biggest heart. I hope you always stay exactly like that, because you are perfect."

Just like a burst river dam, my eyes started flooding my cheeks with tears. "Thank you, Mom. I love you. Sorry it's been so long since I was able to say that." I hugged her tightly then asked her to put the necklace on.

"Well, look at us. This time last week you two hardly spoke. Now we are sobbing at the kitchen table, like old times. Major progress, "Andrea said proudly.

"Yeah, it's a shame it took the equivalent of a volcanic eruption for us to be honest with one another," I said, trying to lighten the mood.

My mom smiled at me and took my hand in hers again.

"You really need to stop crying, Ami, or your eyes will be puffy for your date tonight!" Alison's little head popped around the door frame.

"What is with this child being more clued in than me?" I laughed.

My mother's face lit up. "Is it with that boy from yesterday? The one I was less than welcoming to? I'm very sorry about my behaviour. I should have been kinder, given how he stood up for my daughter. What he must think of me."

"Nana! His name, for the hundredth time, is Yungrae. He's so nice. You should meet him…"

Andrea covered Alison's mouth to stop her rambling, before guiding her out of the room. "I think it's time that you rejoined your brother in the living room, Ali. Stop getting involved in adult conversations." Andrea returned immediately and pulled her chair up as close as possible to me. "Right, tell me. Is this the big romantic night you were planning?"

I briefly explained the conversation I had with Junseo this morning and how I had to come up with a different date night entirely. I didn't want to just sit in the apartment.

My mom looked less than impressed while I was speaking. "Amelia, that sounds like a lot of responsibility to take on. You guys are only starting out. It should be easy and natural, not all these rules and restrictions."

"I know, Mom, but this is something more. I can't explain it to myself. I am willing to take the risk. I've already been down the other road, and we all know how that worked out for me. I have to start trusting myself and others again."

Mom nodded in agreement.

"Amelia knows what she is doing, Mom. Once you see them both together, you will totally understand. They are meant to be. They just fit together." Andrea was demonstrating badly with her hands.

"OK.OK. I understand. I liked how he stood up for you, Ami, so I want to help. What can we do?"

I was so surprised. "Well, if either of you have an idea how we can have a romantic date that is secluded and still exciting, please feel free to share."

They both went silent for a few moments.

"What about doing something at Mom and Dad's house?" Andrea piped up.

I shot her the dirtiest look.

"Oh, yeah. Right. You want romance, not awkwardness."

Mom sat with her lips pursed together, lost in thought. She eventually spoke. "What about taking your father's boat for the evening? It's at the private dock near our house. You have everything you could need, on board. You could always cook for him, and we can pick some nice wines from the cellar at home. You could just text him the address to get dropped at. A bit like the scene in your favourite movie, 'Some Like It Hot'. Very romantic." I didn't have the heart to tell her that Tony Curtis' character posed as the owner of Shell oil and pretended to own the yacht in order to seduce Marilyn Monroe's character in that movie. It was most definitely not similar, but it was a great suggestion.

"Mom! You're a genius. That would be perfect. I love that boat!"

"OK. I'll nip out to the hall and call your father to make sure."

Andrea's excitement was starting to get the better of her. When she spoke, her voice was so high pitched, it hurt to listen to her. "Oh my god, I'm so excited for you! Have you booked in with Madelyn? You're in desperate need of a blow-dry. How about waxing? You'll want that, just in case things heat up later!" My sister was the queen of being inappropriate. I spent more time rolling my eyes at her then I did look at her.

"Oh my god, Andrea, please. That's the last thing on my mind right now. I have so much to prepare, and I have to be in the salon at two! Please don't put me under any more pressure!"

She was smiling intensely in my direction. "Oh, get a grip! You know we will help you! What do you want to cook? He loves steak, right? You're a pro steak-cooker!"

"Yeah, he seems to. He talks about that a lot, actually. That seems straightforward, too."

My mother joined us, once again, in the kitchen. "That's all sorted, Ami, love. I'll stop by the vineyard on the way home and pick you up some nice wine. Do you want something for pre-dinner cocktails as well? Maybe some of the vintage reserve Jameson? We have a crate of that left in the warehouse." For people who didn't drink much, my parents supported my appreciation for Irish whiskey.

"That sounds fantastic, Mom, thanks."

"No problem, my love. I'll give the place a good once-over when I'm dropping it all off for you — make sure you have everything you need."

"Yeah, Mom. Sounds great. You head off now and get started. We haven't got all day. Amelia, what are you wearing?" Andrea was almost pushing my mom out the door at that point.

"I have an outfit in mind. Want to see?"

"Hell, yes!"

We said our goodbyes and parted ways with our mother, before dashing up the hallway to my room. I pulled out the black and white, off-the-shoulder, Balmain dress and showed it to my sister.

"Oh, my good god! That is divine. I'm obsessed with it. What shoes?"

"I bought shoes in Balmain, too." I took the black, leather, Stella sandals out of their box.

"*Epic*. I love it. I'm only weak for the dress, Ami. It's very 'Cruella de Vil' vibes."

I was thrilled to get positive feedback. I loved how the dress hugged my body, and I felt very confident in it. I looked at my reflection in the mirror. The bruise on my neck and knuckles were all I could see. I turned to ask Andrea what I should do, but she was already digging through my accessories.

She pulled out a black choker. "What if you wore this? It may not completely cover it all, but it may disguise it."

I took it from her hands. "You're a genius, Andy." I kissed her cheek.

"Right, well, that's that sorted. What about your underwear. Has to be sexy."

"Jesus Christ, Andrea. Can we not have any boundaries? You might as well come on the date as well!"

She burst out laughing. "I'm sorry, I'm just happy for you. I remember when David and I first started seeing each other. It was so exciting."

I rolled my eyes. "All right, OK! I appreciate your help, but let's not get carried away." I lay out my clothes on the bed beside my sister.

She was smiling shamelessly at me. "You're so cute today, Ami. What should we do now?" I knew she was just trying to encourage me.

I checked my phone to see if Yungrae had texted me back. It was 11.50 a.m. "Shiiiittt! The morning is flying by. Will you come grocery shopping with me, Andy?"

"Of course. Let's get the kids and go. I can bring you to the salon and drop the shopping off at the boat, after."

We hauled ourselves and the twins into the car in a matter of seconds. The rest of the afternoon came and went just as fast. I soon found myself lying on the bathroom floor in a state of panic. I still hadn't heard from Yungrae. What the hell was I going to do? I managed to somehow muster up the courage to call him after realising that staring at my phone wasn't going to get me very far. Surprisingly, it took me a long time to come to that conclusion. It must have rang six times before he eventually answered.

"Hello? Yungrae? It's me... aaahh... Amelia. How... how are you?" I stuttered my way through that sentence.

"I'm fine, thank you... and you?" He sounded so unenthusiastic. Almost rehearsed.

"Well, I'd be doing better if you had texted me back earlier!" I blurted.

"Ah, yeah! Umm... sorry. I'm sorry about that. I just needed time to sort my head out!"

"And how is your head now?" I asked, unsure if I wanted to know the answer.

"I'm fine. Today has just really made me consider a few things I didn't want to all along. I want to talk to you in person as soon as its possible."

I started to feel a bit pissed off. My negative thoughts started to cloud my mind, and I imagined him ending things with me before they had even begun. *How dare he do that to me when I've just started to grow attached!*

"Well, that's great, as I've spent the *entire* morning preparing our date for tonight. I'm sure you can wait to speak to me then! I'll text you the time and where to meet me. I appreciate you answering my call. See you later!" I hissed, and hung up promptly.

I was a little hurt by the scenario I had just illustrated in my head. I also felt stupid for being so emotionally invested in someone I hardly knew. I mean, we had hardly even kissed. What did I expect, a marriage proposal after a few days?

"Get a grip!" I shouted at my reflection in the bathroom mirror. If he was going to end things with me, I was going to make damn sure he would regret it. I had to look my best when he saw me.

The deeper I went into the negative frame of mind, the more pissed off I got. I don't know why the thought of losing him made me so upset, but I do know that whatever happened next, he was going to have a night he would never forget.

I got ready aggressively, listening to the playlist Yungrae had made for me, huffing and puffing as I went along. The contemplation of songs made me angrier, because each song reminded me of how much I was starting to like him. I didn't realise how stressed I was until I saw how tightly I was gripping my blusher brush and how rough I was applying it to my cheeks. I was also extremely nervous about being alone with him. I wanted everything to be perfect, especially after the last few days.

My outfit was placed carefully on my bed, and after I finished my makeup, I started to put it on. I loved the feel of the fabric on my skin. Balmain was one of my favourite brands. I loved the silhouettes the clothes created.

I stared at myself in the mirror once I was ready. I wondered if the past version of myself that existed two years ago could see me now, what she would say. Would she be proud of the progress that I've made or judge me for impatiently rushing into the arms of someone I barely knew but had intense feelings for?

As I smoothened out my dress for the hundredth time, I caught a glimpse of my hands. You could still see the bruises on my knuckles. I couldn't wait until the horrid purple marks faded away, along with the memories of my past. Well, at least, I hoped they would. I didn't want to dwell on that time of my life any more. I wanted to be the person I was when I was around Yungrae. I wanted to be the person he seemed to see instead of who I saw when I looked at my reflection.

I checked the time on my phone. It was time to leave. I had to get there early and prepare dinner and drinks. I grabbed my Louis Vuitton overnight bag and headed for the front door. I stopped for one final check in the hallway mirror. *Come on, girl. Get it together. It's just a date,* I told myself, as I recognised the worried expression on my face.

I closed the front door behind me. The butterflies in my stomach were frantically flapping about. I hoped and prayed that I had picked the right outfit. I was considering different scenarios in my head when the elevator doors finally opened on the ground floor. I immediately spotted Yungrae and the others sitting in the lobby with an older man. My heart dropped, and I immediately held my breath. *Do I talk to them? Do I ignore them?* I thought what Molly would do in this situation. Her voice echoed in my head. *Walk with your head held high, and pretend you're the most powerful woman on this earth!*

I hung my bag over my elbow, popped on my sunglasses and strutted past them. "Good evening, gentlemen," I said with a smirk, as I glided past them, loving the sound my heels made on the marble tiles.

All six men stood up and bowed their heads slightly in my direction. I only relaxed when I reached the car. My heart was racing from that encounter. I definitely felt more confident, replaying their facial expressions in my mind.

I was just about to begin backing out of the car park when a message came through on my phone: ' *Wow!* You sure know how to make my heart race. I've gone up to get ready. I'll be there as soon as I can.'

I responded simply: 'Don't you dare be late!'

I put the car in reverse and headed in the direction of the dock. My heart pounded in my chest all the way there, my white knuckles gripping the steering wheel as if this was a life and death situation. The butterflies in my stomach almost gave me motion sickness. I had to keep giving myself little pep talks to try and calm my nerves, but there is only so many times you can tell yourself, 'You got this,' without it being weird.

I must have been really caught up in my nerves, because I honestly didn't remember the journey. It was as if I blacked out. I'm so lucky I didn't hit anyone or cause an accident. It was probably best not to dwell too much on that, actually. I didn't want to give myself any more anxiety than I already felt.

As I gripped the rope banister to walk on board, I envisioned myself tripping in my heels and falling into the water. This idea made me roar out loud with laughter, like a mental person. I stopped immediately in my tracks and removed my heels. Just about carrying everything inside, I dropped my bag on the white, suede couch and slipped into my Balenciaga sliders.

"Right! Where the hell do I begin?" I slapped the palms of my hands together and darted in the direction of the kitchen.

My mother and sister had literally prepared everything for me, even setting the table. By the time I had the aperitifs laid out and the dinner on to cook, I had about twenty minutes until he arrived. I mixed myself a drink and brought my things to the bedroom. I unpacked, touched up my makeup and checked and rechecked my appearance in the bathroom mirror. I sprayed myself with my favourite perfume and headed back up. He should be here any minute. I wanted to put my heels back on but decided against it, as the water was kind of choppy, and I really didn't want to fall on my ass if the boat rocking went against me.

I glanced at the clock. He was now five minutes late. What if he changed his mind? I panic-downed my drink and went to make another one. Another ten minutes passed and still no sign. The whiskey was definitely making me hot-headed, and I went in search of my phone to call him. I found it on the bathroom sink and saw the fifteen missed calls and twenty messages from Yungrae. I immediately called him back.

He answered on the second ring. "Amelia, I'm at the location you gave me, for the last twenty-five minutes! Where the hell are you?"

Shit. He sounded colder than earlier. "Ah, Sor… sorry. Sorry…" I realised the alcohol had slightly gone to my head. "I'll be right there. Just give me a moment."

I hurried onto the outside deck and called for him. I couldn't help but smile stupidly when I saw him. He wore black, fitted suit pants and a black, satin shirt underneath his black, embellished blazer. His dark, wavy hair parted slightly in the centre of his forehead contrasted against his pale, smooth skin. I almost forgot how beautiful the man was. The moonlight reflected on the water and lit up his face as he approached the boat.

As he got closer to me, I began to feel light-headed. His presence, especially in this setting, was intoxicating. I was in big trouble tonight. I wanted him so badly.

"There you are! Why didn't you answer your phone?"

His tone quickly ruined my good mood and brought me back to reality. He was mad at me, and I wasn't imagining it this time.

"I was thinking the worst had happened. I was screaming your name, and there was no answer from you. What the hell were you doing?"

I lowered my head, pouted and folded my arms across my chest. "I left my phone in the bedroom. I was busy with preparations. I'm sorry."

He had finally joined me on board. He placed his hands on either side of my face and lowered himself until we made eye contact. "You're too adorable when you sulk. I could never stay annoyed at you."

He placed his lips on mine and kissed me without warning. I melted into his kiss and wrapped my arms around his waist, pulling him as close to me as possible. I could only then begin to sympathise with drug addicts. This euphoric feeling was worth losing myself to. I would give everything up to feel this way as often as possible. He was a high I would happily chase forever.

He pulled away eventually and hugged me tightly. I could feel his laughter rebounding against my body.

"Let's at least eat first."

He was always the one to put the brakes on. I was starting to worry that maybe he didn't want me, but then he stood back and looked at me, head to toe, while licking his lips. "You look incredible. I hope you know how hard it is for me to stop, but we both need to eat. I have a feeling we will need all the energy we can get, for later."

He winked at me, and I couldn't help but smile. If he even knew what kind of thoughts were going through my mind right now. I found myself biting my lip.

He placed his hand on my chin. "Stop that, please. I want to be the one to bite that." He brushed my lips with his thumb.

"Right! Come on, before we both end up naked!" I said with a giggle.

I took his hand in mine and led him inside. Food first. Kissing would come later.

Chapter 12

I made Yungrae a drink while he chose the music. He put on Frank Sinatra. Usually that type of thing would make me uncomfortable, but I was in such a little romance bubble that I didn't care and found it sweet. I was obviously smiling hard at him.

"What?" he asked, almost confused by my expression.

"Nothing. It's just not what I would have expected," I teased.

"You bring out the worst in me." His gummy smile made my heart want to burst.

I handed him his drink and headed back to the stove. I sipped my drink while frying the steaks to perfection on the skillet. I was swaying my hips to the rhythm of the music when I felt his hands on my waist and his breath on my neck.

"Careful! You wouldn't want to ruin your dress." He tightened the bow on my apron, playfully brushing against me before giving me space again.

"No harassing the chef, please." I snapped the kitchen tongs in his direction.

He threw his hands up in defence, laughing at the warning I gave him.

I turned my back to him once more. "So, what did you want to talk to me about, anyway? You seemed really off form earlier, but you're fine with me now." I glanced at him over my shoulder to see his reaction.

He remained unfazed by my question. "We can talk about that after dinner. Let me enjoy this a little longer."

His words stung a little, but I chose to go along with his wishes. I didn't want to ruin the mood too soon, either. "OK! That's good, because these bad boys are ready. We can let them sit for a minute while we bring all the side dishes to the table."

His eyes lit up, and he immediately began bringing the food to the table. We sat across from each other while eating. He told me about his day and how a man from their company came to visit them to help them with the media interest. He said he would be staying in the area while the boys enjoyed the remainder of their vacation. I tried my best to enjoy the moment but found myself in a negative haze of dread. I couldn't stop thinking about what he had to say to me, and I nervously sipped my wine. My glass was emptying faster than I would have liked, but I was desperately trying to relax. I sat and watched Yungrae devour everything that was put in front of him.

He caught me staring at him. "What? Have I food on my face?" He looked concerned, wiping his mouth with the napkin.

"No, I was just admiring you. You look happy and relaxed. It's nice." I realised I was drunk at this point. I didn't really even know what I was saying. "Once you're finished, I'd really like to talk about earlier today. Junseo came to chat with me… as you know. And I would just like to say…"

"Don't, Amelia, please. Don't finish that sentence. I don't want to know what you have to say. Please. Please let me enjoy tonight, at least, before you…" He had lowered his head, and he was staring at his hands on his lap.

"Before I what, Yungrae?" I pushed him into finishing.

"Before you end this."

I was smiling at this point.

His face showed complete horror. "Are you laughing?"

I didn't realise I was giggling to myself. *Fucking alcohol!* I got up and sat on his lap. He was looking at me in disbelief.

I wrapped my arms around his neck for support and locked his gaze. "I thought you were coming here tonight to tell me that you wanted nothing more to do with me." I laughed at how ridiculous that sounded out loud.

"What?" he replied.

"Yeah. I really thought you spoke to Junseo and decided that I couldn't handle all this, and I was angry at the thought of you not trusting me, or doubting how strong I am. I can handle anything. I'm amazing, really," I said, giggling again.

"Well, yes, I know you…"

"And another thing," I interrupted him, rudely. "I like you too much for the amount of time I've known you. It just doesn't make any sense, but I'd go to the end of the earth for you, and well... for this..." I planted a kiss on his mouth.

He reciprocated only momentarily before pulling away. "Amelia... are you drunk?"

"Slightly drunk, yes. Majorly relieved, also. I want you so badly that I'm willing to sign my life away. I hardly know you, in theory, but I've never felt so strongly before. I can handle everything that life throws at me with you by my side. I want this and everything that comes with it. Good, bad, everything. Just sign me up." I was swinging my arm over my head.

He caught my loose hand and held it to his chest. "Are you sure?"

"I've never been so sure and unsure of anything," I replied.

He pressed my hand flat over his heart. "This is all you need to be sure of. This is yours. Nobody in the world will ever be able to say that. And in hard times, I need you to remember: this beats for you, and you alone. Please take care of it."

Before I knew it, my hands were back around his neck, placing his ear to my chest. "Same goes for mine. No one can make it pound harder than you can, and even though it's in my chest, it's yours as long as you want it."

He brought his mouth up to meet mine and kissed me softly, at first. I found myself getting lost in the kiss, like his lips were the only thing that could hydrate me after a month in the desert. I wanted more. The rhythm increased, along with the passion, and before I knew it, my legs were placed at either side of his lap. He moved his mouth from mine, onto my neck, and then began gently biting my shoulder. I pulled on his hair, and he growled against my skin. I moved my hands to his jacket which I removed between kisses, and then began unbuttoning his shirt in a desperate attempt to remove the thin layers of fabric between us.

He stopped only for a moment to ask, "Are you sure?"

I nodded then bit my lip. "Let's go to the bedroom."

I stood up and led him down the hallway to the candle-lit room. He took off my dress, sat back on the bed and finished taking off his shirt. His eyes watched me unhook my bra, and he ignored it falling on the floor. I walked over and straddled his lap once more, kissing him deeply this time, as if to convince him of how badly I wanted him. He rolled me onto my back and began kissing me again. The feeling of his skin on mine was even more incredible than I could have imagined. Our bodies connected as if they were now one.

The euphoric feeling lasted for hours until I eventually fell asleep in his arms. It was definitely worth waiting for.

When I eventually woke from the deepest sleep I'd ever been in, I couldn't find Yungrae. It was still dark outside, so I assumed he couldn't be too far away. I quickly threw on my red, Agent Provocateur, silk camisole and matching shorts and hurried upstairs. I didn't come across

Yungrae in the kitchen or living area, so I continued out onto the outside deck, only to find him sitting there with a glass of whiskey and a writing pad. As I got closer to him, I noticed he had his Air pods in and was scribbling on the paper frantically. I was worried that I may frighten him, so I decided to try and get in his eyeline and allow him to spot me first.

His face lit up when he saw me, the troubled expression leaving his face. He removed his headphones before speaking. "Hey beautiful. You didn't sleep for long."

He put everything down and reached out for me. I went towards him eagerly and he pulled me onto his lap, burying his face in my neck. I could smell the whiskey on his breath.

"How long have you been out here by yourself?" I asked, creasing my brow with concern.

He looked up at my face and brushed a hair out of my face with his fingers before answering. "I watched you sleeping for about thirty minutes, and I was feeling inspired, so I came up here to write some lyrics for this song I've been working on. I produced the melody a while back, but I hadn't been able to come up with lyrics good enough, until now."

I leaned towards the A4 pad to try and get a closer look at what he had written. "I hope it wasn't me snoring that inspired your music."

He pulled me away from his work. "*No!* You're forbidden to see or hear anything until it's finished. It has to be perfect."

I sighed, rolled my eyes, picked up his glass and threw back the rest of his whiskey.

He smiled and wiped the residue from my lip with his thumb and then placed it in his mouth. "After all, it was your words earlier that inspired me. I couldn't sleep without taking down some notes. Thanks for this, by the way. I found it on the desk." He held up the note pad after closing it.

I desperately wanted to snap it out of his hand and rip it open to see what he was working on, but decided against it. I wanted him to be able to trust me with things like that. And I had to trust that he would let me hear the finished product when he felt ready to. "OK, Mozart. I'll leave you to it, then." I got up and turned to leave.

"Wait! Where are you going? Are you going to sleep again? You should rest!"

"Me, sleep? While you're out here alone? I'm far too jealous of the moon to leave you alone with her. She's shining on you so lovingly tonight."

I panicked at how weird that might have sounded. I wished I could have taken it back. He looked at me, stunned. I was afraid to know what he was thinking.

"That was so beautifully put, Amelia. You have a way with words. Mind if I use that?" He began scribbling again.

I was blushing in embarrassment. "Sure. I'm going to get you another drink. I'll be right back."

He nodded and continued writing. On my way back to the kitchen, I thought about Yungrae's effect on me. I liked how he made me feel. I filled two glasses and grabbed a pencil out of the writing desk before heading outside once again.

I handed him his glass. "I would like some paper, please."

He looked up at me, slightly confused. "Why?"

"I'd like to write something, too. I'm also feeling inspired."

He handed me a few loose pages, with a big smile, the confusion still present in his expression. I watched him for a few minutes before placing the pen to the paper. I wanted to tell him how I was feeling.

I wrote:

'Dear Yungrae,

I know the time we have known each other hasn't been that long, and ordinarily I would never let someone into my heart. I have to protect myself all the time, and it's been exhausting living with my walls up so high. You have become someone very important to me in such a short space of time, and I truly can't thank you for coming into my life. I am excited to see where things will go for us. I hope that I will be in your life for a very, very long time, because I can't imagine doing this without you. You make me feel so safe in a world of chaos. It's like I've known you forever. I'm struggling to put it into words because I don't understand this feeling myself, if I was to be honest,

so I'll use the words from one of my favourite books. *'It is not time or opportunity that is to determine intimacy; — it is disposition alone. Seven years would be insufficient to make some people acquainted with each other, and seven days are more than enough for others."*
— Jane Austen

It might be far too early to say this, but I love you.

Forever yours,

Amelia'

I put down the paper and immediately checked the time. It was four thirty a.m. My eyes were heavy, and I just wanted to sleep. I knew we had to head back to our real lives in a matter of hours.

I walked over to where Yungrae was sitting and handed him the folded paper. "Don't read that until the right moment."

"And when exactly am I supposed to know when the right moment is?" he replied with a deep laugh.

I placed my hand on his heart and said, "You'll know in here!" I took his hand in mine and pulled him into standing up. "Come on, handsome! Let's get some rest."

I lead him inside and cuddled up next to him in the bed. It wasn't long before we were both fast asleep.

I woke up hours later to the smell of food coming from upstairs. I hurried up there, in a trance from the aroma. The sun was blazing outside, but it was the sight of him that really brightened up my morning.

149

"Morning, handsome. What are you making? I'm actually starving."

He greeted me with the biggest gummy smile. I shuffled over to him and kissed him deeply. He wrapped his arms around me, pulling me deeper into the kiss.

When our lips finally parted, he smiled again. "I wish every morning started like this. I'm making omelettes. Is that OK?"

I nodded so enthusiastically that he laughed at me. "Juice?" I asked, pouring myself a glass.

He shook his head and pointed to a tall glass filled with ice and black coffee. "I always start my day with an iced americano, but I mightn't need to. Seeing you gives me just as much energy," he said, while skilfully whisking the eggs.

I walked up behind him and buried myself in his back with a hug.

We spent the day together, just hanging out by the water. I swam while he napped on the upper deck. The time went too fast. Eventually it was time to go home. I had to prepare for Olivia and Molly's arrival, and he had to return to his friends. I gathered my things reluctantly and we loaded our stuff into the car. Yungrae could come back with me, but only because it was dark.

We talked all the way back to the apartment block. He reminded me of our little creative exchange at four a.m. that morning. I couldn't believe I had forgotten all day. Embarrassment set in, and I felt my cheeks burning up from inside.

He laughed at my discomfort. "Don't worry, I didn't read it. I promise I won't until the time's right!" He pulled his phone cover off to reveal my letter. I couldn't help but smile. He kissed me as if to reassure me then pulled away. "I'm keeping it with me always, until the time is right. Now, I better slip in before you. Once you're settled in, I'll come up to say goodnight. OK, beautiful?"

I nodded and watched him slide out of the front seat before pulling out my phone to send a voice message to my girls.

'Hey, my lovelies! I'm just after pulling into the courtyard now, after the best date I've ever been on. It's far too early to say it, but the feelings are strong, you guys. I can't wait for you to meet him. I hope you're getting organised to come here, and I hope saying goodbye isn't too hard. I miss you both so much. Get plenty of rest between now and then, because you will need it. Talk soon. Love you.'

I sent a text to my mom and sister:

'Just arrived home now. I honestly had the best night. Thank you both for your help. I really appreciate you both. Let's go for a coffee tomorrow, and I will tell you all about it. Love you. xx'

I was just about to get out of the car when my phone vibrated. It was a text from Yungrae.

'I'm inside the lobby with Junseo, Taehwan and our manager. Apparently there were some suspicious guys hanging around outside the building last night. We assume just stupid paparazzi, so don't worry. We've got this covered. I'll meet you upstairs later.'

I checked my makeup before hopping out of the car. I was almost around to the open boot when I felt something strike me in the face. I put my hand to my mouth only to discover blood coming from my swollen lip. Then almost like lightning, another blow came to the back of my head, knocking me onto the ground. I heard the familiar evil laughter from above me. I tried to crawl away from the car but was struck again, this time on my legs. The burning pain began to overtake me, but I kept trying to drag myself away. I could see Yungrae inside the building, being held down by his manager and his friends. He was kicking out and swinging his arms to try and get them off of him. I decided to focus on Yungrae. I could feel the hot blood filling up in my mouth, making it hard to breathe. I tried calling out for him, as I received blow after blow to my body. I tried to protect my face with my hand, but my attacker continued to hit me. I didn't have any strength left to keep moving, so I just lay there, looking at the love of my life, both of us helpless to circumstance. I kept my eyes open as long as I could, but the pain became unbearable, and the blows became more frequent and violent. I didn't want to give into it, but I could no longer stay conscious. I allowed the darkness to overcome me, and I slipped into a peaceful place, far from the pain I felt seconds earlier.

The last thought I had to myself was about Yungrae. I whispered, "I love you. I hope I see you again in our next life."

Chapter 13

Yungrae

As I sat in the lobby of the building I was staying in, I kept zoning out from the conversation that was taking place between my friends and our manager. I didn't really care, if I was honest. All the things that used to scare the shit out of me no longer mattered. All that mattered to me was that woman.

I watched as she hopped out of her car. I couldn't believe I was lucky enough to call her mine. Last night had been one of the best nights of my life. I was looking forward to many more of nights like that. I had been searching for so long for someone with a soul as beautiful as hers — one that complimented mine. No other hand fit into mine as well as hers did.

I watched as the breeze gently blew her hair from around her face, the streetlights highlighting the sparkle in her blue eyes. She smiled at me from across the carpark.

Before I could even exhale, I watched as a dark figure swooped up from behind her and struck her in the face. I couldn't believe it. I watched as she touched her mouth with her hand, and before I could come to terms with what just happened, she was struck again. This time she fell to the ground. Taehwan watched the whole thing unfold and was cursing under his breath. I jumped up to go to her but was restrained. I kicked, screamed, pulled and lashed out with all my might to get away from my so-called friends and our manager who were holding me down.

They were shouting, "This is will harm you more than you know. Don't be stupid. This will ruin your image."

My manager was pinning me to the cold, hard tiles. I writhed from underneath them, thrashing my arms and legs around, in a temper. I saw Taehwan's expression as he looked at me, and then at her being beaten repeatedly by the hooded figure. He immediately released me and Junseo followed suit.

"This is my fucking fault. I have to help her. Get the fuck off me now! I mean it, Manager; if you don't let me fucking go to her now, I'll leave this group in a heartbeat. We have to fucking do something. She's someone's daughter and sister. *Get the fuck off of me!* I will kill each and every one of you if you don't let me go."

I managed to knee my manager hard enough to hurt him, and his grip loosened enough for me to force him off of me. I hurled his body off mine and dashed towards her. Taehwan and Junseo followed close behind me. I swung for the hooded figure, my presence startling him. My fist made contact with his head and that unbalanced him a little. He lashed the wooden bat in my direction, but I managed to dodge it. Taehwan caught it and pulled it from his hands, pulling him forward in my direction. His hood fell off, revealing his face. I would recognise that bastard anywhere. It was Amelia's ex-boyfriend. Richard.

I almost began frothing at the mouth with anger. He was dead. I would kill him for hurting her. I threw punch after punch until he was lying flat on the cobblestone. I kept hitting him in the face until I was pulled up from behind. He was no longer moving. The red mist began lifting and I remembered Amelia. I rushed to her side. I picked up her head and gently placed it on my lap. She was no longer conscious. Her body lay limp on the cold ground. My beautiful girl, beaten and covered in blood. How dare anyone lay a finger on someone so precious, someone so kind and sweet? Would I see her smile again?

The tears building up in my eyes finally surfaced, and I began bawling my heart out. My precious angel lay on my lap, her blue eyes hidden under swollen, purple eyelids. I watched as the ambulance and the police arrived. I watched as they handcuffed and forced him into the car. I watched as Amelia's parents arrived, and her body was rolled onto a stretcher and put in the back of the ambulance. I watched as the paramedics checked her thoroughly. I watched as the police took statements from everyone. I continued crying. I couldn't stop if I wanted to. The salty tears burned my eyes, but they kept flowing as I saw my love being taken away from me. The only thing that brought me out of my thoughts was the familiar soft voice of Andrea, Amelia's sister.

She placed her arm around my head and pulled me in her embrace. "There is nothing else you could have possibly done. You saved her. She will know that. We have to be strong for her. She needs us."

I cried hard onto her shoulder. David's hand was on my back, trying to comfort me. People I hardly knew were here when I needed it — supporting me, giving me hope.

I felt another hand on my shoulder and pulled myself together enough to turn around and face the people calling my name. It was Amelia's parents.

Her mother grabbed me and wrapped her arms around me. "Thank you. I will never be able to repay you for saving her. For standing up for her. For being here. For being you," she said between sobs.

Her husband placed his hand on my shoulder and squeezed it hard repeatedly. "It will be fine, son. Don't worry. She is so strong. She will fight this."

I didn't know what exactly to say as I stared into the eyes of a man trying to hold it together for his family, but I recognised the pain in his expression. We both adored Amelia. As I stared into his eyes, there was something else I recognised in the eyes of the man that I had just met. It was pure hatred and anger. Something told me Richard wasn't going away that easy. Something told me that he would make him suffer, and I would help him in any way I could.

The only thing I could think of saying was, "He will pay for hurting her. I will make sure of that."

He nodded and said, "Don't worry! That boy will die roaring, as long as I have anything to do with it."

David joined our conversation, placing his hands on both mine and Amelia's father's shoulders. "What do you need us to do, sir?"

The three of us made eye contact and began nodding. Whatever was to happen, all of us would die for her.

Amelia's mom interrupted. "Can you all keep your hormones in check for five minutes? We have to follow Amelia to the hospital. She will need us to be there when she wakes up!"

"If she wakes up," her father spat.

"Are you serious? She's our baby girl. She's a fighter. Look how much she has overcome in her lifetime! You think this will be the end of her? We reared her. She will be fine. I know my baby, and she won't give up that easily. Get yourselves together. She needs us."

I turned to walk away, knowing my place. She needed her family. I wasn't needed now.

I wasn't gone ten meters when I heard her mother call after me. "Yungrae! Where the hell do you think you're going?"

I spun on the spot to face her. "She needs her family right now. I don't want to get in the way!"

"Yungrae, if you are not there when she wakes up, she may never forgive us. You're in this now, whether we like it or not! We also need each other. Will you come to the hospital with us?" She stretched out her hand.

I looked towards my friends and my manager who was on the phone, furiously arguing with someone. The boys nodded, as if to say 'Go'.

As soon as our manager caught wind of my plan to accompany Amelia's family, he began panicking even further. "Please, Yungrae! Please! You don't need to get involved any further than this. We are lucky the media haven't got wind of this incident by now. If they do, our PR team will be ready to release a statement saying that you stopped the assault of a local woman. They will make you the hero, but if you are somehow tied to that girl, it will ruin your image. And it's not just you! What about the others? You will be putting them in jeopardy as well! Don't be selfish. There is a whole world of beautiful women out there. Don't fuck up everything you have worked so hard for, over some random one."

The rage began building up inside me again. I wanted to hit him, but I managed to control myself. "Don't you dare speak about her like that!" I spat.

I was about to lose my cool when Taehwan piped up, "Manager! With all due respect, we were the ones holding him down. We should be ashamed of ourselves. If we had done the right thing and stopped him sooner, Amelia wouldn't be this badly injured. What if she... you know... dies because of us. We could have helped her, but we didn't because off our reputations. That is disgusting."

Junseo placed his hand on Taehwan's shoulder. "We are just as bad. We will deal with the consequences when we are called to. Go to the hospital. Be there when she wakes up. She needs you. Manager and I will have a little talk about our options. Please don't worry about it."

Amelia's mother looked concerned but reached her hand out to summon me to join them. I looked at my friends and turned towards the car. I never looked back at them. It was too painful. I had never turned my back on them before. I had never put anything else before them or my career. I knew the risk I was taking, but my heart was telling me that I had to be there for her. I didn't want her to wake up thinking I had left her.

I didn't realise I was crying again, until my tears started dropping onto my hands, both of which I was staring at. A soft hand reached over and placed itself on mine, squeezing gently. I looked up and met the equally worried eyes of Amelia's mother.

"She will be fine. Don't you worry."

I nodded unconvincingly in agreement.

"Thank you for loving her." She squeezed my hand again before turning away.

It must have been obvious to everyone how I felt. I swore to myself, as the car was pulling up to the hospital, that not a day would go by that Amelia wouldn't hear me say those words, regardless of what happened next. I had waited a long time to find her. I could never let her go.

The hours that passed felt like months. They ran test after test. She was scanned and examined meticulously. Luckily her injuries weren't life-threatening, and the doctors were certain that she would make a full recovery.

It seemed like an eternity since they had taken her for x-rays. I waited as patiently as possible, my heartbeat ringing in my ears as I tried to remain as calm-looking as I could on the outside.

When Amelia was finally brought back up to her room, the relief was almost worth celebrating. She was still unconscious, but the doctors had informed us that they would expect her to wake up soon. Her bruising had gotten much worse. I couldn't believe what he had done to her. Why anyone would want to hurt her was beyond me.

I convinced her parents to go home and get some rest, and I would stay here in case of a change. They eventually agreed and left, somewhat reluctantly. I promised to call as soon as something happened. I lay on the bed next to hers and watched her lying there, so perfectly still. The only indication of life was the rise and fall of her chest and the steady pace of the heart monitor that beeped softly in the background. At first the noise was deafening, but once I got used to it, it was almost comforting. I fought as hard as I could to stay awake, but after some time I fell asleep.

I was woken up gently by Amelia's mother who had come in early the next morning.

"I am so sorry. I can't believe I passed out in here."

She fixed my hair with her hand. "It's perfectly fine, my love. I didn't expect you to not need to rest. You would have woken up if she needed you. We can take over for now. Why don't you go home for a while? Shower and change your clothes for when she wakes up."

She smiled so warmly at me. It reminded me of my own mother. I was too overwhelmed to argue with her, so

I got my jacket and headed back to see the boys. I needed to face the wrath of our manager at some stage.

I was halfway down the hospital driveway when I realised I had left my phone behind, so I decided to go back to get it.

I had just reached the room door when I heard her voice. "My lip is burst, isn't it?"

It was like music to my ears. Finally she was back to us. I burst into the room only to find the most confused look on her face. She said the very last thing I expected her to say: "Who are you?" Mom, who is this? Where is Richard? I thought you were ringing him?"

Amelia's mother's phone fell from her hand and bounced off the tiles. The bewildered look on her face matched mine. 'Who are you?' played in my head on a loop. For the first time in my life, I could literally feel my heart breaking.

Chapter 14

Amelia

I opened my eyes to see an ugly, grey ceiling. My head was pounding. Where the hell was I?

"Oh, thank Jesus! Amelia! You're awake!"

My mother shrieked so loudly it almost pierced my ear drums. I sat up, feeling extremely dizzy.

"Jesus, Noel, get a doctor."

My dad darted out of the room. My head hurt so badly, and it took me a few minutes to register where I was. Then I realised I was in the hospital. "What the hell happened, Mom? Why am I here?"

"Ami, there was an incident last night. You were hurt pretty badly." My mother sat across from me. "I must ring your sister, and of course, your boy will need to be notified."

I saw her frantically dialling numbers on her phone. My father rushed into the room, with a doctor in tow. She examined me thoroughly and began asking me questions. I could hear my mom in the background, muttering to my sister. The doctor was explaining to me about my injuries. My right hand was fractured. I stopped listening as soon as

I looked down at myself. This wasn't my body, surely? My thighs were a lot smaller than I remembered. Badly bruised in parts, but still definitely smaller.

"How long was I unconscious for?" I asked.

"About eighteen hours, love," my father answered, while exchanging confused looks with the doctor and my mother. I tried to rip off the neck brace with my free hand. I tried my best to remember what happened, but my head hurt so much.

"Did I do this to myself?"

"No, sweetheart. There was an incident." My father took my struggling hand in his.

"I know. Mom said that already. What kind of incident?" I began, as I went to stand up. I immediately lost my balance and was grabbed by my father.

"Easy, Amelia. You've got moderate brain trauma due to a head injury. You need to give yourself time to recover. Please get back into bed."

I sighed and sat back down. All the motion made me even dizzier. "Is there any chance I could get some pain relief? My head feels like it might explode."

"Certainly, Amelia. I will be right back with something to help, but we will need to have a discussion about the incident, when I return."

I tried to smile at her, but my lips stung really bad. I ran my fingers over my mouth, feeling how swollen they were. I had a cut on the left side, that was super painful to touch. "My lip is burst, isn't it?" I asked my father, who looked devastated.

Before he had time to answer, my room door was burst open by someone. This tall stranger had entered. His dark hair sat messily on his head, and the purple bags under his eyes stood out against his pale skin. He was smiling hard at me. He looked almost relieved. I looked at my parents and then back at him again. I was waiting for someone to explain who he was and why he was here. He began walking towards my bed.

"Who are you?" I asked, looking at him and then back and forth at my parents. "Who is this, Mom? I thought you were ringing Richard?"

My mother's phone fell from her hands and smashed on the tiles. Everyone looked at me in shock.

"What the hell is going on here? Can anyone tell me anything? What the fuck is going on? And who the fuck are you?" I snapped, through my bruised lips.

His face fell, and he looked as if I had cut his heart out of his chest. If I wasn't so confused and my whole body didn't hurt, I would have felt guilty.

"Well? Has everyone lost the ability to speak? What the fuck is the matter with you all? Someone tell me what happened to me. I wake up to find myself in a hospital room with my parents and some stranger."

The room remained silent. I tried hard to remember, but I couldn't. I must have done this to myself. I tried to take my own life and failed. Everyone is too afraid to tell me. That is definitely what this was.

"I hurt myself badly this time, right? You all are too nervous to tell me. I remember being extremely upset after finding out what Richard did to me, but I don't remember feeling suicidal. I'm sorry, you guys. This is my fault." I turned to the stranger. "I assume you discovered me and that's why you're here. Thank you for your help. I'm Amelia. What's your name?"

He couldn't lift his head to look at me. My mother burst into loud sobs.

"Amelia, what is the last thing you remember?" my father asked, taking my hand.

I thought for a second. "Well, Dad, I remember us going to lunch at the bar, like always, and then we both drove separately back to the office. I saw Richard kissing Evie outside her house. Then that's it. I woke up here, then."

All three people were exchanging concerned looks, until my father finally said, "Amelia, honey, that happened fifteen months ago. You've done a lot of great things for yourself since then. Turned your life around. You don't remember the past fifteen months?"

The boy then burst out of the room, not saying a word to anyone. My mother ran after him. I looked at my father for an explanation.

"Amelia, that's your boyfriend, Yungrae. You haven't been with Richard for a very long time. In fact, he is the reason you're here. He attacked you last night on your way home."

The confusion that set in was suffocating. I lay back down on the bed, speechless. How could I not remember any of my life over the last year and a half? Why would Richard attack me? He was the one who fucked up. Tears started forming in the back of my eyes, and my throat started to burn. My head hurt even more than it did before. I wanted to close my eyes and wake up from this, so I just lay there in silence until the doctor came back with pain relief. She could see the distress in my expression.

"Why don't you rest a little, while me and your father have a little chat, Amelia."

I softly nodded and closed my eyes again. I hoped this would soon be over. I hoped that this nightmare would end.

Chapter 15

Molly

I got the call from Amelia's sister in the early hours of the morning. In about four hours, I had packed and was on the way to the airport, getting on the first flight out of New York. My best friend needed me, and I said goodbye to my family a few days earlier than planned, without question. I knew if the roles were reversed, she would do the very same for me.

I managed to get in contact with Olivia just before my plane boarded. She, too, had pushed up her flights and was on the way to help our best friend. I would get there first, as the journey from New York to France was much more straightforward.

I was sick with worry. I was running on pure adrenaline. The flight seemed to take forever. I just wanted to be able to snap my fingers and be by her side. I couldn't imagine how she must be feeling or if she had even woken up. I had asked Andrea to keep us updated on her progress, until we got there.

I got a text from her when I was in the taxi on the way to the hospital: 'Girls, she has finally woken up. Mom said she was very confused, but she is fine. All I know for the moment is that the doctors are very happy with Amelia's progress, and her injuries are moderate. They are confident that she will make a full recovery. Mom hung up on me a few minutes into the call. Where are you both now? Do you need anything? Ring me if you have any problems. — Andrea'

I don't believe in God, but I was thanking him, anyway. The taxi driver seemed to sense my impatience and drove like a lunatic. I all but threw cash at him when we arrived at the front of the hospital building. I grabbed my luggage and hauled ass into the reception. I wasn't looking where I was going and collided with the first person I encountered. The force of our collision resulted in me flat out on the tiles.

"I am so sorry, miss. Are you all right? I don't know how, but I didn't even see you. Please accept my apology." He reached out his hand to help me up.

I was about to release hell on him until I saw the tears in his eyes. My heart took over. "It's fine, honestly. Don't worry about it. I was in my own world. I've a lot on my mind today, too."

His eyes met mine once again. I saw the pain behind them. He lowered his head and began picking up my luggage. I studied him and finally recognised who he was.

"It's Yungrae, right? I'm a huge fan. I hope you are OK. I don't know what has upset you, but I hope it gets a little better soon."

His expression changed to shock. "Please," he whispered. "Please don't tell anyone I was here."

I squeezed his arm gently. "Your secret is safe with me, darling. I got you. Go get some rest. It mightn't seem so bad later."

He nodded and then continued out of the building. I gathered myself and bolted towards the first nurse I met. She guided me in the direction of Ami's room, and I hurried to her side as fast as I could. I knocked on the door but didn't wait for an answer before entering.

As I entered, I saw my best friend sitting upright in her bed. I ran to her and wrapped my arms around her, trying not to squeeze too tight. All the pent-up frustration and worry I had felt began streaming down my face. It was the first time she had seen me cry. She was stiff against me. I pulled away to look at her. The blank expression on her face completely threw me off.

Before I could speak a word, she looked at me dead in the eye and said, "Sorry, but who the hell are you?"

Chapter 16

Olivia

I had never received a scarier phone call in my life, than the one I got informing me of my Ami's condition. Her poor sister was so good to think to call us. My mind has been all over the place, since. I somehow managed to change my flights for later on in the week. I begged and pleaded with the customer service representative until she finally gave in and changed the dates on my tickets. Saying goodbye to my family earlier than planned wasn't easy, but I knew I had to be there for my best friend. She would do the same for me.

After the first connection of my journey, I managed to get in contact with Andrea again. She told me that Amelia had woken up and was seriously confused, but that was all she knew for now. I felt relief that my friend was OK, but also a strange sense of fear for her mental state. She must be in a bad way after dealing with such a traumatic experience. Statistically, most assaults are carried out by people we know well.

I wanted to hug my best friend, and the thought of that, alone, was keeping me from completely falling apart.

I knew Molly would kill me if I didn't stay strong for Amelia. Every time I wanted to ball my eyes out, I would hear Molly in my head, telling me to 'get my shit together'.

Three flights and thousands of miles later, I arrived in France. Molly was meeting me at the airport. She wasn't giving me any straight answers on Amelia's condition, so that was starting to panic me even more.

When I eventually made it out of baggage claims and customs, I spotted Molly waiting outside. She was so well put together all the time. She never had a hair out of place. Sometimes all I wanted to see was her getting a stain on her outfit or something, just to make her seem a bit more human.

I was really taken aback by the Molly who came to meet me. Her face was gaunt and pale-looking, like she hadn't slept in days. Her clothes were mismatched, and she kept fidgeting frantically. I had never seen her like this. The minute I placed her in my embrace, she burst into tears. Things must have been very bad, considering I was the one holding it together.

"What happened, Mol? Is Ami OK? Are you OK? What's going on?" I pressed her for details.

She pulled away and tried to wipe her constant flow of tears. "I'll tell you on the way. Things are much worse than I imagined."

She helped me with my cases, and we hurried towards the car. "Who owns the wheels?" I asked, as Molly brought us to the trunk of a car with no driver.

"Amelia's parents loaned it to us! I'd ask you to drive, but you're terrible, and it's the opposite side of the road here."

"Molly, I would like to point out that you have never seen me drive, so how would you know?"

"I've seen you cycle a bike, and that in itself is enough danger for pedestrians."

I laughed and shrugged in agreement. "Come on! Let's get out of here. I want to see her."

Molly stayed very quiet at the start. I wanted to let her gather herself before putting her under pressure to talk to me, but the silence was deafening. "

OK, Mol! Give it to me straight! How bad is our girl?"

She sighed deeply. "Olivia, I don't think there is an easy way to say this, but when I went to see her, she… didn't… recognise me." She barely made out the last few words.

"OK, well, she has had major trauma and was unconscious for eighteen hours. That is understandable. Of course she didn't recognise you at first. What did she say when she came around? Did she remember the attack?"

I could see Molly's grip tighten on the steering wheel. "No, Olivia. She doesn't remember the last fifteen months."

The blood drained from my face. "What? So she doesn't remember…" I trailed off.

"She doesn't remember even meeting us, Olivia, and the doctors don't know when, or if, she ever will."

I looked at Molly before bursting into floods of tears. And it was in that exact moment I lost all faith in everything I had ever believed in.

She spent the rest of the car ride filling me in on everything. How Amelia had spent all this time with a guy called Yungrae, how they became very serious very quickly, and how she now didn't remember him either. She told me that Amelia wouldn't go back to the apartment because she didn't want to stay with strangers. She told me how worried her parents were, and they kept begging us to help jog her memory.

By the time we had reached our accommodation, I had heard just about enough. I wanted to drown myself in alcohol, while researching everything I could on memory loss after head traumas. I was so bewildered by this news that I couldn't even appreciate the apartment.

"I need a stiff drink, Molly." I took out my laptop and started to get to work. We spent hours researching and taking notes. We would do anything we could to help our friend. Anything at all, for her.

Eventually Molly stood up and announced, "I have had enough for now. I can't take in any more information. I need some fresh air and a pizza. And you're coming with me!" She peeled my hands of the keyboard and dragged me in search of food.

We began making our way home after eating our body weight in cheese and dough. Just outside the apartment door were four boys, waiting patiently for us to return. They introduced themselves, one after the other, and asked if they could come in to chat. They explained that Yungrae had packed his things and that he was uncontactable. They were worried for their friend and wanted to know if they could help in any way. Molly pulled out a bottle of whiskey, and we all brainstormed ideas. We talked about our friends, and they told us how Amelia and Yungrae seemed like they were mapped out in the stars. I was drunk at that point and didn't want to ask for clarification on that statement, so I decided it meant 'made for each other'.

We talked and drank until the small hours of the morning until we called it a night. Molly and myself dragged our sorry butts to bed and passed out immediately.

When we woke up around two p.m., any hope that had remained at bedtime had well and truly evaporated. I went to Molly's room the second I woke up. She was in the bathroom, throwing up. I couldn't help but feel a tiny bit of pride. That was normally me.

"The universe is truly out of whack," Molly said, when she finally could bring herself to come out.

"You're starting to sound like me," I smiled at her.

"Ugh. I know. I'm losing my edge," she said, before wiping her mouth with the back of her hand.

We gathered ourselves and headed for the kitchen for sustenance; anything that would help the state we were in. On our way, we noticed the other room door open. We looked at each other as if we were thinking the same thing:
Did she come home?

We rushed into the room to find Junseo and Taehwan snoring in the bed. Bitterly disappointed, I shook my head and sighed. Molly, on the other hand, turned her disappointment to pure rage and began shouting that it was time to get up. She sounded like a dying cat. The boys were in complete disbelief.

"Molly. What is wrong with you? I almost went into cardiac arrest," Junseo said, after springing from the bed.

"Who said you could stay here? Why would you do that?" she growled, and hurled a cushion at him.

Taehwan was now sitting on the floor beside the bed, peering over the top of the mattress, in fear of Molly's wrath.

"What do you mean? You begged us to stay," Junseo challenged her.

Molly couldn't answer. I was too unwell to think of anything useful to say.

The only thing that broke the silence was Molly's sobs. "I'm so sorry. I got a fright. I thought Amelia had come home. I wanted it to be true."

I hugged her as tight as I could. Junseo walked over to us and wrapped his arms around the both of us, and seconds later Taehwan did the same. The reality was harsh, and it hit us harder than the hangover.

"We have to try to remain positive. Everything will be fine. It will all work itself out," Taehwan said unconvincingly, when our eyes met.

"I know. All we can do is live in hope that we get both our friends back soon."

The four of us showered and changed not long after that and headed to the café near the apartment for breakfast. We parted ways around noon, and Molly and I went to visit our friend at her parent's house, something we continued to do every day for a week. It was very uncomfortable at first. Amelia said very little and made us feel very unwelcome. Her mother tried her best to encourage us to keep coming back. The Amelia that would greet us, was cold and angry. She wasn't the girl I met in Japan. The girl who when she wasn't entertaining us with her sunshine personality, had her head always buried in a book. The girl who brought you home flowers when you were sad and cried with you. After the first few visits, Mollie would come home and cry. That, in itself was overwhelming. While waiting for a light at the end of the tunnel, we found ourselves spending more and more time with Junseo, Taehwan, Jiseok and Daeshim. We had a great time together but always agreed it wasn't the same without our friends. There was always something missing. The days flew by and still no major progress. We got a laugh out of her, here and there but still no sign of our Amelia returning to us. We still lived in hope that one day she would.

Chapter 17

Amelia

I spent the last week being forced to hang around with strangers. My parents were convinced that this would bring back my memory. They spent every minute of every day watching my every move. It was exhausting. Maybe my memories would never come back. What was so bad about that? If the last fifteen months were worth remembering, why would I have forgotten them? Molly and Olivia seemed very nice. There was no denying that, but how could they expect me to force a friendship with them?

I was due to leave again in three weeks, and I had absolutely no intention of going to Korea. I think my parents wanted me to, which was the weirdest thing ever. Imagine moving to the other side of the world! Apparently I had already lived in Japan for this past year, but even seeing the pictures didn't convince me that I did. I knew myself. I wasn't strong enough to leave everything behind to start a new life in a new country without my family. I laughed to myself every time they brought it up. We couldn't be as close as they kept saying we were. I mean, they clearly didn't know me like they said they did.

I couldn't stop thinking about Richard. Why on earth would he try to kill me? I just didn't understand, and honestly, I just wanted to see him for myself. I planned to sneak out today and go to the prison to see him. I just had to be clever. I told everyone I was really tired and a little overwhelmed, and that I wanted to lie down for a while. I waited for them to leave the front zone of the house. I grabbed Dad's car keys that I had stolen earlier and bolted at the first given opportunity.

The sat nav brought me right up to the prison gates. It was creepier than I could have imagined, but I needed answers from Richard. I needed to know what had happened and why. I was brought into the visitor's room after being searched and questioned thoroughly. He was brought out to me a few minutes later. He looked badly beaten. His bruises almost matched mine.

He sat in front of me with the biggest smirk on his lips. "I knew it would only be a matter of time before you showed up. We can't keep away from each other, right, Pugsley? I have to say, I like the new look. Purple always suited you."

I smiled back. "Your handiwork, apparently."

"I hope you're not too mad at me. I had to put you in your place. That's always been my job, right, babe?"

I searched his black eyes for some small bit of remorse. "They say you could have killed me, you know. You might be losing your touch."

He laughed, and then stopped before answering. "I could have, yes. I would have, too, if it wasn't for that wanker getting in the way."

I didn't even flinch when he mentioned Yungrae.

Richard smiled wider this time. "What's the matter? Did that wanker get bored of you, too? You weren't good enough for him, anyway. No one wants to play with broken toys."

I didn't react. I just continued to stare at him, desperately trying to jog my memory. I must have zoned out, because he kicked me in the shin under the table.

"Please don't tell me you're fucked in the head now, too? How can I tease you if you're too stupid to banter with? I suppose I should take credit for that, too. After all, how many times did I hit you in the head?" His smile was wider.

"I wouldn't know. I can't remember, actually. I have no memory of the last fifteen months. That's why I came to see you. I wanted to remember, but I can't."

He started chuckling hard. "That's just fucking made my day. Only I could do that. I took all your memories from you. Ahahahahahaha. That's fucking beautiful. I love that. I am sad about one thing, though." He grabbed my casted hand, pulling me forward.

I tried not to scream in pain. "And what's that?" I was barely able to ask.

He came as close as he could and whispered, "That you can't remember how hard I went on you. I did almost kill you, and I enjoyed every second of pain I caused you.

You're nothing, and that's what you deserved. You thought you won the day you left me, but look at you now. All those marks on your disgusting body were caused by me. I ruined you."

I managed to free my hand, and I was furious. I couldn't understand what I said next. "Yeah, sure. It's a shame I don't remember all that, though. That could have been anybody," I sniggered at him.

As soon as I finished that sentence he got up and lunged at me, causing me to fall over. He was standing over me, laughing, when I heard my father scream, "Get away from her. You sick bastard!"

All of a sudden, I remembered seeing Yungrae as I fell to the ground that night. I remember Richard laughing and receiving blow after blow. Then nothing else. Just that boy's face. My father picked me up, and I watched as the guards pulled Richard away, still spitting nails as he left.

"Jesus Christ, Amelia, what were you thinking coming here? Are you OK? Are you hurt? We should go to the hospital."

I started sobbing. "I'm so sorry. I'm so sorry. I just wanted to remember, so badly. I feel like everyone knows so much about me, and I have no idea what they are talking about. I am trying my best, but nothing was working. This did work a little. I remembered something. Only a small memory, but I saw Yungrae as I fell to the ground. He was trying to get to me. To help me, I guess, but I have no idea why."

My father looked relieved and concerned as he pulled me in for a hug. He hadn't hugged me like that since I was a child. "Please stop forcing this. It will happen when the time is right. Let's go home. Your mother and your friends are worried sick."

I walked hand in hand with my father until we were out of the building and safely in the car. I glanced over my shoulder as we pulled away and vowed to never see that man again.

Chapter 18

As my house arrest and around-the-clock supervision continued into the following week, I was running out of ideas on how to entertain myself. I wandered around my parents' garden, wondering if things would ever be different. Could I trust the people in my life? They were convinced they knew me, and that left me more confused than I had ever been in my life. They filled my head with stories that I had been a part of but couldn't remember. I trusted them only because I saw pictures of myself with them. At first I wondered if they could have been forged. The version of Amelia that they seemed to love was a stranger to me. I hadn't known her like they did. The only connection I shared with her was our remarkable resemblance. I liked the sound of the girl they described, but she didn't feel remotely related to me.

I couldn't stop thinking about Yungrae. I remembered the fear in his eyes and how hard he fought to get to me. Even still, I felt nothing. I wanted to, though. I wanted to be free of this torment.

I walked the entire perimeter of the garden a few times and then decided to go further rather than retrace those footsteps again. No one seemed bothered enough to stop me, either. I kept walking until I reached the edge of the water, where my father's boat was docked. I hadn't been on it in ages and was somehow drawn to it. I couldn't explain why. I decided to check to see if the doors were open. I couldn't explain my curiosity, but something inside me told me to go inside. I fiddled with the door handles, expecting it to be locked, but to my surprise they both swung open. It looked the same as always. It even smelt the same, like pipe tobacco and fresh linen, if that even makes sense.

I came to an abrupt halt when I noticed the sweatshirt draped across the couch. I picked it up to examine it. 'Fear of God' was printed across it. It looked familiar. Maybe it was David's? I smelt it for further inspection. It smelt so familiar, but it definitely wasn't a scent that I could connect to someone I knew. I placed it down carefully and continued strolling aimlessly around the inside. I noticed little things, like a glass drying on the sink, and the food in the fridge was still in date. This made me curious. Was someone staying here recently?

I ended up downstairs and at the door of the master bedroom. The door was slightly open. I wandered in to find more clothes strung across the bed, floor and other furniture in the room. I was definitely convinced there was someone squatting here, and I didn't feel like hanging around to find out who. I turned to leave, when I spotted an iPhone on the floor in front of me. The screen was smashed to pieces and the phone cover barely hanging on. I decided to take it as evidence.

I carried on leaving until I saw a man, outside on the top deck, walk past the window. I ducked down and began crawling.

"Why the hell am I hiding. This boat is my father's." I said out loud to myself.

"Yeah. Why are you hiding? More importantly, why are you even here? Your parents said no one would disturb me. I guess they don't keep their promises, either."

I looked up at the owner of the shoes directly in my eyeline. It was Yungrae.

"OK! Firstly, I had no idea you were even here, and secondly, I went for a walk and ended up here, for some reason. I don't know why."

"Perfect. That's just fucking perfect, isn't it?" he stammered.

"Are you drunk, Yungrae?"

"Yes. Why are you still on the fucking floor?" He reached out his hand to help me up.

"Good question." I didn't know why I was still crouched down on all fours.

He started walking away from me as soon as I got back up on my feet.

"Hey. Where are you going?"

"To get another drink. You coming or what?"

I followed him to the kitchen where I found him with his head buried in the fridge. "Well, that's just fucking incredible." He pulled a wine bottle from inside and turned it upside down to show that it was empty.

"There's more on board. Come on, I'll show you." I led him down the narrow hallway, holding him by the wrist.

"If you're taking me to the bedroom, I would just like to note that I don't really feel up to being molested right now."

I stopped and turned to face him. "*Seriously?*"

He shrugged and smirked at me. "I'm kidding. Relax."

I showed him the storeroom and opened the door to show him the stash of expensive wines. "What are you in the mood for, then? Shiraz, Cabernet, Pinot Noir? What are you thinking?"

He didn't look at all impressed. "Surprise me! You're good at that."

"Stop taking little jabs at me, please. This isn't my fault. I want to remember. I even went to the prison the other day to try and jog my…"

He grabbed my shoulders before I could finish. "You did what? Jesus, Amelia! What were you thinking? Why on earth would you visit that prick, after what he did to you?" He clenched his jaw. I looked into his eyes then at where he had placed his hands on me. *Why did I like this?* He immediately let go and swallowed hard before walking out of the room. "Yungrae wait! Please!" He stopped and turned to face me.

"I wanted to know what happened, and I wanted to see if I could recall *my* version, not everyone else's."

We were now both wedged at either side of the door frame. Our bodies were almost touching but not quite. The tension was most definitely undeniable. I found myself starting at his lips, wondering what it would be like to kiss him, and I wondered if that would reinstate my memories.

"Stop doing that. It's not fair." He stormed off, after snapping the bottle from my hands.

I followed after him like a lost puppy. He didn't speak for what seemed like an eternity. I was the one to break the ice. "But I did remember something."

His eyes remained on the glass in front of him. "I suppose you're going to tell me?"

I ignored his sarcasm. "I remembered seeing you and falling to the ground. I remember being in pain, too. Lots of pain, actually."

He spun around to face me. "You remembered the worst part. Why couldn't it be us meeting, or your friends? They meant the world to you."

"I hope that someday soon I will, but for now I'm stuck like this." I dropped my head in shame. "I'm so, so sorry."

"What on earth are you apologising for, Amelia? None of this is your fault. That's just typical of you."

"Well, I feel really guilty. I'm not stupid. I can see I am hurting you, and I can't stop. This is not fun for me."

"I know, I'm sorry, but I'm leaving tomorrow anyway, so you won't have me to burden you with guilt for much longer."

"Your leave… leaving?" I wasn't expecting that answer. Where… where are you going?"

"Home, Amelia. There is no reason for me to stay here, any more."

I couldn't explain why this upset me, but all I wanted to do was cry. "So I won't see you again?" My eyes filled with tears.

He shrugged. "Probably not, no. It's for the best."

I didn't want him to go. I was just getting to know him. "Well, let me at least make you something to eat. I have a feeling you're drinking on an empty stomach."

He slumped down at the table. "Fine. I don't have the energy to argue with you right now."

I went about preparing dinner for us both. Upon closing the fridge, I had a flashback. "We did this before, on this boat… right?"

He kept his head lowered, red eyes on his glass. "Right. The night before the 'incident'. We stayed here together. You cooked for me. It was one of the best nights of my life."

"I vaguely remember. You helped me bring the food to the table."

His eye's widened in my direction. "Yes. I did do that. You stood at the stove cooking, while I watched." He got up and pulled an apron out of the cupboard. "You wore this." He placed it over my head and spun me around to tie it. He grabbed my hips gently and steadied me. He whispered in my ear, "I told you to be careful not to ruin your dress."

His breath on my neck sent electrical currents up my spine. I liked this. I stood, watching the water boiling. Pasta was on tonight's menu. Nice and simple. He pulled away from me and sat down at the table again. He became very quiet. I then saw him fiddling with something shiny in his hands.

My curiosity got the better of me. "What's that?"

He looked up at me. "I wanted to give this to you before I left. I got you this necklace a while ago. I wanted to give it to you when we both left for Korea, but it looks like it's just me now."

"Can I see it?" I took it from his hands and began looking at it. "It's beautiful. I love the stone in it."

"It's opal. It reminded me of the flowers we saw in that garden in Eze. I thought you could have it to remind you of home."

I went to sit beside him, but I took the phone from earlier out of my pocket first and placed it on the table without thinking.

"Amelia? Why have you got my phone in your pocket?"

"Oh, yeah. Sorry about that. I was taking it as evidence of a squatter on the boat. What happened to it? The screen is mangled, and look, the cover is hardly hanging on."

I picked it up to prove my point when the cover separated from the phone and a piece of paper fell out. I picked it up immediately, as I saw my handwriting on the outside. "What is this?"

"You wrote it for me the night we stayed here. You told me to only open it when the time was right. I actually forgot it was there. I stupidly listened to you, and I still don't know what it says."

I looked at him. "Let's recreate the moment I gave it to you. Maybe it will help."

He led me to the upper deck and sat down. He told me I had sat, writing it, on the other side. I took the piece of paper and read it to myself. The last really affected me. I found myself reading it over and over.

'It might be far too early to say this, but I love you.

Forever yours,

Amelia'

I remembered feeling really strongly when I wrote it. Suddenly I remembered being there. I remembered him and I that night. It was all starting to come back to me.

"Yungrae! I gave this to you! Yes, I remember now." I began walking towards him.

"What? You what?" He stood up immediately.

I grabbed his face in my hands and began kissing him before he could say anything else. The feelings all came rushing back. I couldn't believe I almost lost him. We continued kissing until the tears started flowing down his cheeks.

I pulled away and began crying too. "Yungrae, I'm so sorry it took me so long. I can't believe this."

He smiled and pulled me into his embrace. "You came back to me, and that is all that matters. I am so happy. I love…"

I covered his mouth with my hand. "No, please don't finish that sentence. I need to read this to you first."

"OK." He pecked my lips and sat down before pulling me onto his lap.

I read out the note. I turned to face him before telling him, "Yungrae, I love you."

He kissed me over and over and over again. I hoped he would never stop. When we finally did, he placed his hand on my face, gently caressing my check with his thumb. "I love you too, Amelia."

I kissed him once more, pulled his head on my chest and squeezed him against me. "Baby, let's eat something. I'm hungry now," I said.

"OK, my love. Whatever you want to do is fine with me."

We went back inside and ate dinner together. After eating, I knew it would be time to call my parents.

My mom answered on the second ring. "Amelia, where the hell are you now? I hope you are safe."

"I'm fine, Mom. Calm down. I'm down on the boat with Yungrae."

"Oh, OK. That's good. Anything there jog your memory?"

"Yeah, Mom. Everything is starting to come back to me."

"Oh, sweetheart, that's great news. I am so happy for you. I will tell your father now. Have you spoken to your friends?"

"Not yet. I think I'll talk to them tomorrow. I'm going to stay here tonight, though. We will come up to the house for breakfast in the morning. If that's OK."

"Of course, sweetie. No problem. I'll see you then. Enjoy. Tell Yungrae that I said goodnight."

"Night, Mom." I hung up my phone and turned my attention back to Yungrae.

"You're staying?" His gummy smile widened.

"Yeah. Is that OK with you?"

He grabbed me and pulled me into him. "Of course. Let's stay forever."

"OK. Let's stay forever," I laughed.

He picked me up and placed me on the kitchen's island, so I was at eye level with him. He didn't say a word, but I knew exactly what he wanted and needed. I kissed him deeply to express that I, too, felt the same. He slipped my shirt up over my head and threw it behind him. He then gently kissed every bruise and mark on my upper body. His lips met mine again, while he unbuttoned my jeans. After pulling them off, he kissed every bruised part of my lower body. He then picked me up and took me to the bedroom, where we stayed until morning came. I was finally back in the arms of the man I loved, and nothing felt better than that.

Chapter 19

Last night was amazing. I loved waking up beside Yungrae. I loved his messy bed-head and his voice when he first woke up. I could do this forever.

"Do you really have to go home today, or can you stay a little longer?" I asked, as I started to walk around the room, picking up various items of clothing.

"No, I can stay until the weekend. I can go back with the others then."

"OK, that gives us a little more time. Great. It won't be long until we join you in Seoul, anyway."

He jumped up out of the bed. "You're going to come? You haven't changed your mind?"

I looked at him with disgust, "Of course I'm coming. I'm not giving up on that opportunity. I worked hard to get a place in that school, and I love teaching. Jobs in private schools like that don't come up that often."

He picked me up and spun me around. His gummy smile melted my heart.

"This is the best news! I am so happy," he exclaimed.

"Me too, my love. I'm really excited!" I kissed him all over his face. "Can you loan me some clothes, please?"

"Yes, take whatever you want. What's mine is yours."

I pulled on a pair of his cargo pants and an oversized T-shirt. I helped him pack up his things before we went to the house for breakfast with my family. My parents were so happy to see me that I almost got away with my outfit.

"Amelia, honey, what the hell are you wearing?" My mom looked appalled by my outfit choice.

All I could do was laugh. We sat and ate together, and it felt so good being there, all together. My sister, her husband and the kids arrived in time to eat.

I figured this was the perfect time to tell them my plans. "Guys, I just want to thank everyone for being so patient with me and helping me get back to somewhat normal. I can never repay that kindness. I would like to take this opportunity to let you all know my plans going forward. I am still going to move to Seoul in the coming weeks. I hope you can respect and understand my decision. I am very excited for this new journey."

They all exhaled at the same time, as if they were holding their breath.

"Well, thank god for that, anyway. I hoped you would do the right thing. I am proud of you," my dad announced, making me giggle.

"Honestly, Ami, we were hoping you would say that, because we already booked our flights to come for Christmas," my sister admitted.

I burst out laughing, and everyone else joined in. The rest of the morning went so well. It wasn't long before we were saying our goodbyes, and I was trying to talk myself into going to see my friends. I knew that wouldn't be easy.

Yungrae took my hand while I was lost in thought, staring at the front door. "Everything will be fine. Stop worrying. They are your friends. They completely understand."

"I know you're right, but I'm still nervous. I wish they made 'I'm sorry I forgot you existed when I had amnesia' cards."

"You'd need a lot of them," he joked. I shot him a dirty look.

We eventually got organised to go and face my friends. The closer we got to the apartment, the more nervous I got. I let Yungrae out a block away, and I continued on my own in the car. The butterflies in my stomach were becoming unbearable.

I mustered up enough courage and walked in the front door. "Hello? Anyone home?"

No answer. I wandered around the entire apartment to find no one there. Even the rooftop was deserted. I threw myself down on the couch in frustration. I would just wait until they got back.

They had to come home eventually. Ten minutes later there was a knock at the door. I jumped up to answer it. It was Yungrae.

"No one is at home? Is Molly and Olivia here?"

I shook my head. "Nope. No sign of them. I guess I should ring them."

He nodded in agreement.

I took out my phone and dialled Olivia's number. She answered cautiously. "Hello. Eh, hello. Amelia, did you call by mistake?"

"No, I called you on purpose. I just popped into the apartment to say hi, and you guys are out?"

"Oh, really, OK. Is everything all right? We are just out on the water with Yungrae's friends. They hired a boat. We will be home around seven. If you're still there, maybe we will see you then."

She was being so cold towards me. I wished I could just hug her. "OK, Liv. Would you like if we made you something to eat when you come home?"

"*We*? Who is we?"

"Yungrae is here with me. Ask the others too, if they would like to join us."

"Ami?"

"Yes, Liv?"

"Are you back?"

"I'm getting there. Everything started coming back to me last night. It's still a little foggy in places, but I hope I'll get there."

I could hear her start crying on the other end of the phone. "We will turn around and come straight back. Let's just order in tonight. See you both soon."

"Olivia?"

"Yes?"

"I love you."

"I love you, too".

I flopped down onto the couch again. Yungrae joined me. "So, how many are we having to dinner?"

"Everyone. Your friends and mine. They rented a boat together. They are going to come back soon, and we can order in something later."

"When did they even become friends?"

"Who knows?"

"Maybe they bonded over having shitty friends like us."

I playfully slapped his shoulder. "Please don't make me feel any worse. I'm tired, all of a sudden. I kinda want to have a bath and nap." I got up and walked towards the bathroom, stopping in the doorway. "Well, are you joining me or what?" I turned to see his reaction.

He didn't flinch. "I don't really want to watch you have a bath, Amelia."

I took his shirt off of me and threw it to the floor. "Who said anything about watching?" I said with a smile.

He got up slowly, not once taking his eyes off of me. "Well in that case... race ya!"

He bolted past me. I tried my best to catch up with him, but he beat me there. The anticipation was overwhelming. He kissed my shoulders while I carefully locked the door behind us. I knew it was about to be my turn to win.

We slept for a lot longer than I had wanted, and we ended up being woken by the voices of Molly and Olivia, screaming my name from the front door.

"I'm in my room, be there in a minute!"

Not a minute after I gave up my location, they burst into my room. They both jumped on top of Yungrae and myself, laughing uncontrollably.

"Sorry for interrupting, but we are here for our best friend," Olivia said, kissing my cheek. "What were you both doing in bed in the middle of the day, anyway?"

"Making up for lost time, eh?" Olivia gave Molly a dirty look.

"Molly, could you be a little more sensitive? Our girl and Yungrae have had a hard time recently."

I giggled like a little child. I was so happy to have the three most important people in the world to me, in the same room, finally. "I'm really sorry for my behav..."

Olivia covered my mouth with her hand.

"Don't even dream of finishing that sentence, Ami. None of this is your fault," Molly scolded me.

We heard male voices in the hallway.

"We are in here, guys," Olivia shouted.

The four boys entered my room and began buzzing around Yungrae. There were now eight people in my bedroom, laughing and joking with one another. I looked around at my friends, old and new. It made my heart feel full. Yungrae caught me watching them and began kissing me passionately, pressing me into the pillows. They all started making noise to signal their discomfort, until they got up and left the room.

He didn't stop until he was sure they had gone. He pulled away slightly and fixed the lost strands of my hair. "I knew that would work." He was smiling down at me.

How I loved that gummy smile. "I love you."

He smiled even wider before kissing me softly. "I love you too, Amelia."

I wanted to reside in that moment forever, but I knew we couldn't. Our friends were waiting on us.

"We'd better get up, my love."

It was like he read my mind. "I know, but promise me something first?"

"Anything for you."

"Stay here tonight? I like the idea of making up for lost time." He rolled back onto the bed, covering his face with his hands.

"Ahhhh. Please don't say things like that to me. It teases me, and I am weak when it comes to you." I pulled his hands away and dragged him onto his feet. "Come on. Clean thoughts only. Our friends are waiting."

I kissed him and went into my closet in search of clothes. I pulled on a pair of black, Skims bicycle shorts and a crop top to match. I loved the soft, stretchy fabric. It was so comfortable.

We went and joined our friends in the living room. They had one of their music videos playing on the TV and were arguing over who was the most handsome of the group. I looked at Molly, who rolled her eyes at me. Yungrae sat down, and I cuddled up next to him. Jiseok turned to ask my opinion.

"My bias will forever be Yungrae. Sorry, boys."

They all gave out to me. Our evening turned out to be one of my favourites so far. We ordered in Chinese food and played board games. I didn't realise how competitive Molly could be. I was a little afraid of her and Junseo. They were getting very heated over a game of monopoly. It was entertaining to watch, though. I think she had a soft spot for him, but she would never admit it.

We called it a night around one a.m. The boys went back downstairs, and Yungrae went to bed before me. I wanted to chat to the girls before we went to sleep. Olivia made us a camomile tea each, and we sat at the kitchen table. I was trying to find the right words to say to them. I wanted them to know how much I appreciated them.

"First off, just let me say thanks. I don't know how to repay your patience and kindness this past week or so. I honestly don't know what my life would have been like if I couldn't get my memory back. I am still not one hundred percent, but I am trying hard to recall them all. Every memory with you girls has been the most precious to me, and the fact that my mind erased them for a while..." I broke down crying.

Oliva took my hand, and Molly got up and wrapped her arms around my shoulders.

"I... I... I can't find the right words to say. Forgive me. I can't believe I have something this special. You both came from two different sides of the world to be here for me, when I needed you the most. I don't know how to thank you. I am so lucky to have you in my life," I said, through my sobs.

They both cried with me.

"We said this ages ago. We will always be here for you. No matter what. Always and forever," Molly said, squeezing my hand.

"We're in this for life, girly. There's no getting rid of us," Olivia added.

"I don't think I've ever seen you cry before coming here, Mol," I laughed.

"She's human, after all. Who knew."

We finished our teas and tears and went to bed. I was eager to be alone with Yungrae again. I rushed up the hallway and into my room, only to find him sound asleep. I couldn't help but smile at him. He looked so peaceful. I crawled in beside him and cuddled into his back. I was out for the count, moments later.

Chapter 20

Yungrae and the boys' last few days in Nice came to an end faster than anticipated. As they say, 'time flies when you're having fun', and we had just that. We spent our days by the pool, or out at my parents' house. My parents held a huge family barbecue for us one night. We all sat around the firepit, singing and drinking too much wine. I really loved these people.

They swam in the sea near my house. We took the quad bikes through the vineyards and had a group picnic. We made our own wine and had a tasting later that day. We did everything. I took Jiseok and Taehwan horse riding the day before they left. They promised to take me horse riding when we get to Korea, at least twice a month. The doctors would kill me if they ever found out the activities I took part in with my hand in a cast.

We made many plans for when we got to Seoul, but who knew what they would be actually free to do. They worked harder than anyone I'd ever met, and they hardly ever got time off. I was worried that I wouldn't get much alone time with Yungrae, but he assured me that we would have plenty of time together. I knew it would be hard, but I was excited to see where the journey took us.

Yungrae and I had spent our last night together on the boat. It was beautiful. I didn't want it to end, but I was hopeful that we would have many more nights like that in the future.

We couldn't even see them off at the airport. We had to say goodbye at the apartment. I held on to him for what felt like an eternity. It was so difficult to say goodbye, even though I would be leaving for Korea in just under three weeks. The thought of being without him for a day was hard.

He kissed me one last time before I watched them leave, one by one, and get into their van. I was glad to have Molly and Olivia with me. I wouldn't feel so alone. I wandered aimlessly back to the apartment and up to my bedroom. I just wanted to crawl into bed and sleep. I figured that the more I slept, the sooner it would be time to leave Nice.

When I walked into my room, I found a pile of T-shirts and sweaters folded on my bed, with a note on top. It said:

'Amelia,

I know how much you like wearing my clothes, so I'm leaving some behind for you to wear when you miss me. In return, I want you to send me pictures of you in them. Please stay safe.

I love you.

-Yungrae'

I lay down on top of them and took a selfie to send to him. 'Thank you so much. I love them. Miss you already.'

He responded with a selfie of Daeshim asleep on his shoulder. 'I can't put it into words how much I miss you. Kisses.'

It made me so happy to see him. I put on the top shirt, put away the rest of them and then crawled under my duvet. Molly and Olivia came to the door to check on me.

"Want some company?" Molly asked.

I pulled down the duvet for them. "Always."

The three of us chatted for a little while and eventually fell sound asleep.

My sister rudely woke us early the next morning. She wanted shopping buddies and decided to force us to go with her. We tagged along against our will. I wore another one of Yungrae's T-shirts, over bicycle shorts, to go shopping. I might never take them off. It was the closest thing to having his arms around me.

My sister dragged us from shop to shop and made us watch as she tried on outfit after outfit. As much as I hated it, I was grateful for the distraction.

Thankfully, the weeks flew by. We kept ourselves busy, seeing the sights and spending time with my family. The girls helped me to pack all my things. It wasn't so difficult with the extra pairs of hands. My bruises finally faded away enough to hide with a little BB cream. The last thing I wanted was to go to Korea with my past still all over my face.

I got my cast off just before we left. I was so relieved. I still had to wear a removable splint, but at least I could shower properly.

We finalised everything with our schools and had our apartment all set up and ready to go. I was so excited to actually live in Seoul. It looked amazing, and from the way Yungrae described it, I felt like I would really be at home there. I had five meetings with the school over zoom, just to discuss work-related matters. I found them a little intimating, if I was honest. We signed ourselves up for Korean lessons for when we arrived. I wasn't going to tell Yungrae about that. I was hoping to one day surprise him with my killer language skills. I wasn't quite sure how I could keep it a secret from him, or for how long, but I was definitely going to try.

I took Molly and Olivia up to Eze, too, before we left. I showed them the gardens, and we ate at the same hotel that I took the boys to. We talked about me maybe one day getting married there. They were amazed by the place. I loved that they loved it too. It meant a lot to me being able to show my friends all my favourite spots.

We found a big oak tree at the edge of the village and decided that we should bury our friendship bracelets at the base of the tree. We had gotten them made when we were in Japan, in this tiny little shop we had stumbled upon, one of the many times we got lost. We placed them in a Ziploc bag and then into a metal box and buried it under the tree the next morning at two a.m. I don't know how we didn't get caught. We vowed to all come back here the year we turned fifty and dig them up again.

We shared our predictions on what our life would be like when we all reached that age. I couldn't say for sure, but I was hopeful that I would be happy. That's all I wanted in life. Just to be happy in myself.

On our last night, my mother held a dinner for us at my family's house. It was just perfect. It felt good having mended our relationship this summer. I was leaving feeling lighter. I had battled many demons this time, but I was leaving with a whole new future to look forward to.

When the morning of the day we were leaving came around, I was very emotional. As much as I wanted to go, there was a part of me that would miss my family terribly. Every time I saw the twins, they just got bigger and bigger. Who knew how grown up they would be at Christmas time. I hated missing out on so much of their lives.

My whole family accompanied us to the airport. We needed to bring three cars to fit everyone and our luggage. I hugged each member of my family so tightly. I knew it wouldn't be long until we would all be together again. I was glad I wasn't travelling alone. The three of us being together was perfect. We balanced each other out well.

Yungrae had texted me before I left the apartment:

'Hey baby. I know today will be hard for you, so I just wanted to remind you that I love you and I can't wait to see you. I will meet you at your apartment. I'm looking forward to having you here. I managed to get this weekend off, so maybe we will go away somewhere before you start work on Monday. Safe flight. Text me when you land. xx'

I was looking forward to seeing him, too. I couldn't wait to hug him and feel his arms around me again.

It was time for the final goodbyes. I hugged each member of my family. I had started crying while unloading my luggage from the car and didn't stop until we had gone through security.

The first of our flights was from Nice to Dubai, then we would change and fly direct to Incheon. I said goodbye to my luggage in Nice and wouldn't see it again until we landed in Korea. I didn't know how to feel about that.

The first flight was straightforward and was over and done with quite quickly. The airport in Dubai was extremely busy. It was overwhelming, especially going through security. The made us stand in a narrow tube, while a machine scanned our bodies. It's a nightmare if you're claustrophobic.

Once that part was over with, we decided to look around duty-free and spend money we didn't need to spend. I shouldn't have been allowed to enter a Mac cosmetics shop with a credit card. I did an unnecessary about of damage. I just loved their lipsticks.

After we had worn ourselves out doing that, we went for food and a few glasses of wine while we waited to board our flight. When the announcement was finally made, I was relieved. I just wanted to get into my seat and pass out.

We boarded the plane, and as soon as we took our seats, a flight attendant came over to tell us that there had been a mistake and that we were sitting in the wrong place. I was so tired and confused that I didn't bother to argue with her. I knew we were in the right ones, but she was so persistent that I just gave up at the first sign of an argument. She guided us all the way to the front of the plane and opened the curtain to the first-class section.

I panicked.

Molly tried to clear things up. "Excuse me, miss, there must be some serious mix-up. We are in economy. See, our tickets say right here."

"No, ladies, your tickets were upgraded this morning to first class. Here are your seats."

We said nothing more and sat in our little cubicles. I had a feeling that Yungrae might have been behind all of that, so I sent him a text:

'Just after sitting in our seats, our tickets were upgraded. This is crazy. I hope you didn't have anything to do with it (but if you did, thank you so much). One last flight before I get to you. I'll ring you when I land. Love you.'

It was honestly the easiest journey I had ever made. The comfort was incredible. I would fly all day, every day, if this was how I could do it.

I slept for most of the flight, and while I did, I dreamt of Yungrae. I was obsessed. I couldn't wait to see him. I'm sure I've said that about a million times, but it was true. I couldn't.

We made it there eventually, and I rang Yungrae while we were waiting in baggage claim. "Hey, just waiting on our bags now. Should we get a taxi or the bus or something? What's best?"

"Oh, don't worry about that. I've sent a car for you guys. I figured you would need plenty of space for your luggage."

"Are you serious? You're too generous. Stop spoiling me. It's too much."

"Amelia, I will never stop. This is the least I can do, since I can't meet you there in person. If I was a normal guy, I could collect my girlfriend from the airport myself. When you walk outside, look for a guy holding up your names on a card. That's your driver. He will bring you straight to the apartment. I've already given him the details, but feel free to remind him if you must."

"Thank you so much. You're far too good to me."

"I'll see you soon."

Our bags started showing up in baggage claim and soon after we collected them, we were heading out the doors in search of our driver. Sure enough, there he was, waiting patiently for us. He loaded all our luggage into the huge Mercedes van he was driving. I really didn't know how it all fit, if I was honest. Somehow it did.

Our driver didn't say a word the whole time, until we stopped outside a gated apartment complex; the biggest one I had ever seen in my life. It didn't look like the apartment we had viewed on zoom a while back.

"Sir, are you sure this is the correct place? It doesn't look right."

"No, this is the place. Maybe it has been renovated since you saw it."

Molly muttered under her breath, "Not unless it's been renovated into a whole new building structure and location."

I gave her a dirty look to warn her not to be disrespectful. The gates opened, and he drove us to the third building in the east of the complex. He then began driving into what resembled a multi-storey car park. He pulled up to door on the third floor and started getting out of the car. We followed his lead and got out, although none of us knew what the hell was going on. From the corner of my eye, I spotted Yungrae, Daeshim, Taehwan, Jiseok and Junseo heading in our direction.

I ran to meet them. "What the actual hell is going on, you guys?" I barked.

"Is that how you great your boyfriend after spending so long apart?"

"It was only…"

He kissed me midsentence. Yungrae took me by the hand and lead me off into a long hallway. He brought me to the end of it, and we stopped right in front of 3A. He keyed in a code into the lock and opened the door for me. "Go on in."

I did as I was told. He showed me around the whole four-bedroom apartment before stopping in the living area where the others had joined us.

"We live just upstairs, Amelia. Isn't this great?" Yungrae's gummy smile was wider than I'd ever seen.

"OK, so why are we here then? I'm so confused," I replied.

"We made some arrangements, and this is your new apartment, girls. Welcome home."

I looked at him in disbelief. This was where we would be living — in the same building as them. I could see him easily without having to sneak around. I was at a loss for words. I wanted to argue with him. It wasn't fair that they had done all of this for us. I also didn't want to seem ungrateful, so I just stayed quiet for now. I would speak to him later, in private.

Molly and Olivia were smiling hard. Molly went straight to hug Junseo, and they held onto each other a little longer than normal. I wondered what was happening there. Olivia caught me staring at them, winked at me then mouthed 'later' at me. I was dying to ask questions.

"Thank you all for everything. This place is amazing." I kissed Yungrae's cheek.

He pulled me in for a kiss and continued kissing me over and over again. He began running his hands all over me.

Daeshim started clearing his throat. "Right… OK… That's enough of that, guys. We need to get going."

I reluctantly pulled my lips from his and snuggled into his chest. He kissed the top of my head.

Olivia spoke for me, as if she was reading my mind. "Where are you guys going?"

"We must go into work for an hour. Just to go over some stuff," Taehwan answered.

Junseo and Yungrae exchanged glances. "We would also like to have you over for dinner tonight. Should we say seven thirty?" Junseo asked.

"That would be lovely," Molly answered for us.

Yungrae took me by the hand, into the kitchen. "I know you've got something you wanted to say to me. We can talk about it tonight when we have some alone time. I will leave you to get unpacked and settle in. I hate having to leave you when you've just gotten here."

"It's fine. Go. We can hang out later. I'm looking forward to dinner."

He soon followed the others out of the room. I rejoined the girls in the living room. Their squealing and giggles were the soundtrack to my entrance.

Molly swung her body around to me. "I can't believe we live here, dude. Look at this apartment. It's amazing."

"I know, Mol. We are so lucky."

The three of us collapsed onto the couch just before the doorbell rang.

"Not it!" Molly and I shouted in unison, as loud as possible.

"Fuck!" Olivia growled at us. On her way out of the room, she hurled a cushion at us.

We heard male voices coming from the hallway and allowed our curiosity to get the better of us. The driver, along with another random man, was dragging our luggage into the hallway, when we made it out there.

We decided to play 'rock, paper, scissors' for the rooms, as we couldn't choose. Olivia and Molly ended up with the rooms next door to one another, and I got the choice of the two rooms on the other side of the apartment. I picked the bigger of the two. It had an amazing wardrobe, after all. After unpacking the majority of our stuff, we all went for a nap, before it was time to get ready for dinner.

At 7.25, we loaded our slightly jet-lagged bodies into the elevator, keyed in the special code Yungrae had given us and rode to the next floor. Taehwan opened the door to reveal himself wearing an apron with a female's body in a very tiny, red bikini, on it. He must have forgotten he had it on and remembered only when he saw our confused expressions. His cheeks went redder than the bikini, and he quickly removed it while we walked in past him.

Molly ran straight into Junseo and gave him a kiss on the cheek. I had quizzed Olivia about it briefly, before we got there. She had told me that they had spent a lot of time together while I was 'recovering' (as she so gently put it). Olivia didn't know the extent of their friendship, and we both agreed to not comment until Molly spoke to us directly about it.

I found my boy in the kitchen, armed with a large knife, chopping an onion skilfully. I hugged his back. Daeshim handed us all a big glass of wine and guided us to the table, where we sat for what seemed like hours, eating, drinking and swapping stories.

The evening was going so well — too well, almost. I didn't know why, but I couldn't shake the feeling that something bad was about to happen. I tried to ignore it and swap the feeling with a nice wine buzz.

Eventually I had to go to the bathroom. Naturally, Olivia and Molly tagged along. We had to discuss the evening in private.

While we were en route back to join the boys, the doorbell rang. Olivia looked at me and I shrugged my shoulders. We stood staring at the door, and the bell rang again.

"I'll get it!" I shouted towards the dining room. I guess I was feeling a little brave.

On the other side of the door stood the most beautiful girl I'd ever seen in my life. I was stunned by her presence. Her long, dark hair fell softly around her shoulders, and her pale, flawless skin was complimented by her big, brown eyes and soft, pink lipstick. I smiled at her and gestured her to come in, unsure if she could speak English or not. She graciously glided in past me and was met by Molly's hand, confident as ever.

"Hello, I'm Molly. Nice to meet you."

She responded with an American twang. "Hey. I'm Kim Eunji. Nice to meet you, too." She smiled sweetly at us.

"What brings you here?" Olivia stammered, surprising herself and us all.

Eunji kept her composure. "I'm here to see my boyfriend, Yungrae. His manager said he was home."

My face completely fell as the words left her lips. I stared at her blankly, hoping I had heard wrong. The three of us stood there, speechless.

The only sound breaking through the silence was Yungrae's voice. "What are you doing here, Eunji?" He sounded really pissed off.

"I came to see you. Why aren't you happy to see me?"

With that, I brushed past her and went out the front door. I managed to make it to the elevator before the tears started. The only thing I could hear, in that moment, was Eunji's voice, saying, "My boyfriend, Yungrae", on a loop.

Just like that, my new life was slowly starting to resemble my old one, and I wasn't sure I could survive this time.

Milton Keynes UK
Ingram Content Group UK Ltd.
UKHW011824261023
431404UK00001B/6